Echoes of My Dreams

Lee Phipps

Gray Door Ltd.

ISBN 978-0-9908034-8-5

DEDICATED

To those who are struggling against all sorts of trials and tests, but are still holding on to their faith and trust in God, and especially the "Virtuous Woman" who is standing alone without the help and support of any other, but is still being firm in her stand and commitment to God.

Table of Contents

ECHOES OF MY DREAMS

"I can't start thinking this way," she thought, "This is just an echo of my dreams that I had for me and Carl. I have nothing to build another dream on."

Chapter One: Why can't I remember?

"It's a hand! Of course it is. Why couldn't I remember that?" Very slowly, he roused from a deep sleep. His thoughts were taking a long time to get from one to another. He'd been staring at something, trying to remember what it was. His head was aching something fierce, and when he attempted to turn himself and identify where he was, his brain felt as if it would explode. He relaxed and laid back into the position he'd been in; stretched out, lying flat on his stomach, with one arm sprawled out in front of him.

Then he noticed something else about the hand. It was caked with a dark substance. After studying it for a while, he realized it was dried blood. He also became aware that the hand he'd been looking at was his hand. He moved it to his aching head and felt a place where the blood was coming from. There was a big knot on his head with matted wet hair.

The knot was painful to the touch, so he moved his hand from the wound and allowed the cut to continue oozing blood.

Something above him was making a noise and attracting his attention; causing an attempt to roll over without making his head start to throb again. He wanted to see what was making the noise. Thoughts were coming very slowly, and he had to think a while to recall what it was. It slowly occurred to him that it was a bird singing on the small branch of a tree above where he lay. Where he was lying was in a muddy, shady place under some low hanging branches, a few feet from the water's edge of a small river.

When he started moving around, even though it was slow and slight, the bird flew away.

"Why is my mind so foggy? Why can't I remember things?" he wondered. "These things should be as easy to remember as my name." Then, unexpectedly, he realized that he couldn't even remember his name.

As his cloudy thoughts cleared some, his mind repeated strange words over and over. "I'm going to kill you. I'm going to kill all of you! I'm going to kill you. I'm going to kill all of you!" It was as if he could hear himself saying it. He wondered what it was all about. It was a frightening sensation to not remember who he was, or where he was, or how he had come to be there. What could possibly have been happening that would have him saying something like that to someone?

Evidently there was some sort of altercation between him and some other people; and more than two because it was like he was saying "all of you" instead of "both of you".

'All of them', whoever all of them were, must have overpowered him, and left him for dead.

He felt it would surely only be a short while before he would start to remember.

When he tried to muster up enough strength to roll over onto his back it sent severe pain throughout his body so he didn't even want to attempt to move. He relaxed again on his stomach, and the pain subsided a bit, so he just laid there for a while trying to think.

"This is ridiculous," he thought, "what has happened to me that would make me not able to remember things? I should at least be able to remember who I am." Suddenly he had a thought; why not look in his billfold for his identification to see who he was? In spite of the pain, he forced himself to turn enough to reach into his back pocket for his billfold. Nothing there!! He painfully forced himself to roll over onto his back and pushed himself up into a sitting position. Maybe he carried his billfold in his shirt pocket, or his front pants pocket. No billfold!! In fact all his pockets were empty; there was nothing that could help him remember who he was.

"That probably explains what happened to me," he thought.

"Somebody robbed me, and thought I was either dead or dying and just dumped me here."

He sat there for a while, hoping the pain in his body would diminish. As his body slowly adjusted to the pain he tried to get to his feet. The pain in his right leg just below his knee was severe. Unable to apply much pressure as he stood, he wondered if it might be broken; so he unbuckled his belt and pulled his pants down to examine it. His leg was badly bruised and scraped. It was dark blue mingled with a greenish yellow color, but he decided that it was not broken.

He hoped walking on it would not cause further damage.

He pulled his pants back up and buckled his belt. His clothes were wet more than just from the mud puddle he had been lying in. He wondered what had happened to make them that way. Where he had been lying was very close to a river, though the water in the river was down quite low.

Perhaps he had been thrown into the water, but had instinctively got himself out, and crawled to the spot he had been in.

The thought crossed his mind to get in the river and wash some of the mud out of his clothes; but he was afraid that he might be too weak to contend with the flow of the water, and might not be able to get back out of it.

Surely someone was looking for him, he thought, and the sooner he got to where there were people, the sooner he would be able to find some answers to this mystery.

Beginning to feel a little bit stronger, even though his head was still aching with a dull throb, he looked around and tried to determine what would be the best direction to go to find people.

Probably it would be best to go out the way he had been brought in, he decided, so he looked around to try to find something that would determine which way that would be.

Whoever had brought him to this spot had either covered the tracks very well, or there had been enough wind in the mean time to blow sand over all the tracks. The only other thing he could decide was that possibly he had got up out of the river and came to this spot.

He decided to go upstream on the river. It would be difficult going because of all the brush and trees he would have to go through, but, if he followed the river bed it would be easier he decided. Then he would only have sand and gravel to contend with. It was slow going without assistance because of his bruised leg. He looked for a stick among some of the driftwood that had washed downstream and gathered in a bunch, finding one that was about the right length for him to use to help him walk. He found that it made traveling easier, and a little bit faster.

As he made his way up the river he came to where a small tributary joined the river and contributed its small amount of water to the flow of the river. The water was clear and he found a small pool where the water was still and reflected the blue sky and the puffy white clouds. He had been thirsty, but was reluctant to drink the river water, so he made his way to

the pool and knelt down to drink of the cool clear water. As he bent down to the pool he saw his reflection in the clear water.

There looking back up at him he saw a hollow eyed, scruffy, gaunt and haggard looking fellow with scraggly hair, and streaks of dried blood tracing down his face.

"It looks like I haven't shaved for over a month or maybe even longer, or even combed my hair in that length of time.

Who in this world am I?" He thought. "What kind of life have I been living?"

He felt very disturbed, and apprehensive. He had been praying, but he prayed again, and asked God what he should do. Suddenly, he felt a peace come over him, and it was as if he could hear in his mind an answer, "Just stay cool, I've got this."

"Well, if this is something God is doing, then I guess I shouldn't worry about it. But, I wonder how long it will be before I will know what is going on."

He got a long deep drink of the cool clear water, and it seemed to strengthen him quite a lot. He washed the blood off his face the best he could, and combed his hair with his wet fingers, but as his fingers brushed the knot on his head the sharp pain kept him from touching that spot again.

After what seemed like a long time because of his slow traveling, even though it was a relatively short distance, he came to where he could see a bridge up the river. Several times he had to stop and wait until his head cleared, because he had grown so dizzy he felt like he would pass out.

After sitting on a large rock to rest for a while and regain some of his strength, he made his way on up to the bridge, and slowly ascended to the road.

When he got up on the bridge he could see where there had been a wreck on the bridge. The indications were that it was a one car accident. The skid marks on the bridge showed that the car had suddenly turned and went across the left lane of the highway for vehicles traveling in the opposite direction, and slammed into the side of the bridge. Then the marks left on the bridge railing indicated the car had possibly spun around and almost went up over the railing on the bridge before it slammed back down and came to rest in the lane that traveled in the opposite direction of what it had been going. It might have been possible for someone to have been thrown out of the car and over the bridge railing into the river.

The accident scene had all been cleaned up, but there was still broken glass, and the cement bridge railing was scarred.

He studied the situation, and wondered if perhaps he had been in the wreck and possibly had been thrown into the river. He also wondered that if he had how he had managed to get as far down the river from the bridge and the wreck, to where he was when he awoke.

The water in the river was not real high as far as being full, but he decided that there was enough water, and the flow was swift enough to have washed him down that far before he could have got out. But, since he could not remember what had happened at all, he wouldn't really be able to explain it.

He decided there might be a good chance that he had been in the wreck.

However, if he was in the wreck, that brought up another question. Surely someone would have known he was in the car, and why had no one been looking for him when he was not in or close to the car after the wreck happened? There surely must be an answer to that, he thought, but his mind was just too muddled right now for him to think what it would be.

Feeling very faint and weak, and already exhausted from coming this far, he still realized that it was getting late in the afternoon, and the sun would soon be going down. The sky was beginning to get cloudy and dark, so he didn't know if that might mean rain, but he wanted to get where he could have a roof overhead if possible. He decided to try to find a house, or at least be walking along the road in case a car came by. His body was aching, and he sure wanted to get somewhere so that he could rest where he could also be comfortable, and not have to spend the night lying on the ground. It took him a little while to decide which direction to go.

There didn't seem to be any cars traveling this road. It seemed to be a very remote area. He had expected to have had several cars show up in the length of time he had spent on this road, but so far not one car had appeared.

Limping along for about half a mile or so he finally came to a dirt road leading off the highway. There was a mail box along the road, but he couldn't make out what the name on it was, because of it being faded out, but he decided the road probably led on up to a home. He would follow it he decided, and hoped he was right in his decision.

After going about half a mile on a narrow one lane dirt road, what looked like it might be a barn came into view.

Getting closer it was certain that it was a barn, and he could see the house just a little farther past the barn. Feeling grateful that he was now this close he made his way toward the barn. It couldn't be determined if there was anyone living in the house from this point, but between the house and the barn he might at least not have to spend the night on the ground.

As dizzy and weak, as he felt, he hoped to be able to make it to the barn, and lean on it until he could regain his strength.

"Just a little farther and I can rest," he thought as he stumbled toward the corner of the barn.

Just as he got to the barn and reached out to grab onto it to keep from falling, he saw the barrel of a rifle pointing right in his face, and someone said, "Who are you, and what are you doing here?"

His hand never touched the barn, and he fell, face-first right into a fresh puddle of cow manure. But, he didn't know about it, because he had gone out like a light just as the lady with the gun had spoken.

CHAPTER TWO: All tied up

When he awoke he went through another round of trying to remember where he was, and still couldn't remember who he was; but he did remember finding his way to the barn, and remembered the gun barrel in his face, but only remembered the first few words of the lady asking who he was.

Now he was puzzled, because he found that he had been tied up very tight, and couldn't even scratch his nose that was itching.

He was very uncomfortable with the ropes around him. He couldn't even get into a partly comfortable position. "What is this all about?" he wondered.

The lady noticed that he was awake, and came to the bed where he was lying, and asked him if he was hungry.

Thoughts raced through his mind now, and he thought, "I'll bet she was in on whatever happened to me, and why I was robbed and left for dead. Now her, and whoever she is helping will really finish me off."

"Why have you got me tied up?"

"Well, considering who you are, I just don't trust you; that's why." She answered.

"You know who I am?"

"Of course I know who you are. I know exactly who you are." she said as she very unsympathetically looked down at him.

"Who am I?"

"Why don't you tell me?" She quickly shot back at him. Her eyes narrowed, and she had an unwavering look on her face.

"I can't tell you who I am, because I can't remember who I am." he answered.

"Nice try, Turley. If I was you, I'd try to forget who I was too."

He sort of twisted in the ropes as though trying to pull loose from them and said, "I wasn't trying. But I really did forget. I can't remember who I am, I don't know where I am, and I certainly don't know why you feel that you need to have me tied up."

Suddenly, he realized he was only wearing a pair of shorts.

"You undressed me!" he nearly shouted.

"Of course I did," she said, "I gave your stinking body a good bath too. I wasn't going to put you in my bed with you covered with mud and your face full of cow manure. I cleaned up the outside of you, but only God can clean you up on the inside. If you had any good sense in that bloody head of yours, you would be on your knees asking God to forgive you
 for the things you've done."

She turned and started walking out of the room, but turned back toward him and added, "I also washed your clothes; you can put them back on as soon as they get dry."

He thought about what she said. He almost said what he was thinking, but then thought better of it. He thought back to when he first woke up and realized he couldn't remember, and had decided that whatever the situation was, and whatever happened that brought him to where he was now certainly would be something that he felt he should pray about, and ask forgiveness for anything he might have done that may not have been right. He did pray, and not only asked forgiveness for anything he might have done, but explained how distraught he felt about not remembering. He also asked how long was it going to take before he would be able to remember? He immediately had the thought run through his mind that God had everything in control, and that there was nothing to worry about. It was almost as if God was saying to him, "Just stay cool, I've got this." and his panic seemed to just fade away. However, without knowing what happened he didn't feel he could make any intelligent decision for what he should do, so he prayed that God would give him guidance. "I don't know what I've done," He thought, "but I must have been brought up knowing about God, because that was the first thing I thought of when I heard those words, 'I'm going to kill you, I'm going to kill all of you;' going through my head. I asked God to forgive me for whatever it was I had done. Then all the way while I was making my way to get here I was praying to God and asking Him to forgive me."

The lady was bringing a bowl full of something to feed him.

"What are you going to do with me?"

She sat down on the edge of the bed beside him. "Well, I'm going to feed you some breakfast, although it is already afternoon, but this is about all I could fix up that I felt like you might be able to eat. What have you been doing, going on a forty day fast? You look like you haven't eaten for months."

She scooted a little closer to him so that she could reach better, and continued. "After you've had something to eat, I'm going to get you into my husband's pickup and take you in to the sheriff. And..." closing her eyes briefly as a mischievous smile invaded her tanned pretty face, "it would be nice if there was some kind of reward for bringing you in."

Going in to the sheriff was something that he had thought that he might do because he thought that would be one way to go in finding out his identity, and also alert the sheriff about being robbed of his possessions. But what could be the reason she would take him to the sheriff? He wondered.

"Why would you be taking me to the sheriff?" He asked.

"Well, because the sheriff knows what to do with hoodlums and criminals like you." She said.

"What makes you think I'm a hoodlum and a criminal?"

"Instead of asking me why I think you are, why not ask me why I know you are a hoodlum and a criminal?" she fired back at him.

"I woke up down by the river with no billfold, or money, or anything else in my pockets; a big bleeding knot on my head, and all the signs that I had been mugged and robbed, and you are saying that I am a hoodlum and a criminal?" He angrily tried to scoot his body into a more sitting up position, and continued, "How do I know you weren't in with the thugs that robbed me?"

"Well, you don't know that I was with them, but I do know that you were with the hoodlums that robbed a place, and threatened to kill them, and then had a wreck on the river bridge over on the highway. I have proof of that."

The words that had been going through his mind earlier came back to him when she mentioned the threat to kill that had been made.

"I don't know why you didn't have anything in your pockets, or any billfold;" she continued, and her eyes were almost flashing fire. "maybe so that you couldn't be identified. But, you were in the wreck, and that is why you have the knot on your head."

There was no backing down with this girl. Her mind was made up, and her determination was stirred. It was showing in her face.

He looked at her, and studied her face for a moment. She seemed to be hard as nails as far as her character, but she was a beautiful girl as far as her looks. She was wearing a western style shirt and blue jeans paired with dusty worn cowboy boots. "She looks like a rodeo queen." He thought.

Her soft brown hair reached down just below her shoulders. He decided she was probably still in her twenties, and maybe just her mid twenties even. But thus far she conducted herself in a way that portrayed her as someone beyond her years in knowledge and experience.

It was hard for him to carry on an argument with her; partly because of her beauty, but even more so when he was already convinced that she just might be right.

He decided it would be more in his favor to tone down his dialogue a bit if he wanted to make any headway towards having her untie him.

"You mentioned your husband," he said, "Where is he?"

This question seemed to shake her just a bit, but not noticeable unless someone was paying close attention, so he wondered about her slight hesitation before she answered.

"Never you mind about my husband, he's around here somewhere, but we don't need him to get you to the sheriff."

She put a spoonful of food to his mouth, and added, "He's not going to wonder where I am, I go places all the time and never tell him where I'm going."

He pulled back from the spoonful of cereal. "Do I get to ask God for a blessing on this food before I eat?"

14

"Oh, you are one cool character." She said. "You can't fool me into thinking you are someone you are not. I know who you are, and I know the kind of person you are doesn't ask God to bless the food they eat before they eat it."

"I sure wish you would tell me who I am," he said with a confused tone in his voice, "and just how you happen to know who I am. I honestly don't remember."

She sat the bowl down on the nightstand beside the bed, and got up and went to another room and grabbed a newspaper.

"Alright smart guy, it tells all about you here in the paper."

She sort of shook it at him as she made her way back to the bed where he laid.

He wriggled himself to sit more upright, where he could give his full attention to the girl who was about to tell him who he really is.

"It says that you and three other guys robbed a place, but was unable to get any money except what was in the cash register; so you made everyone in the place give you the money they had. One of you kept yelling at the people to hurry up and hand over their money, or you were going to kill all of them. Then you ran out of the place, and stole an old lady's car, and got all this way away from there before you had a wreck on the bridge over on the river."

She stopped momentarily and looked straight at him as though she expected him to be looking guilty. "The other three guys were killed. Evidently you were very lucky. You must have ran away from the wreck so the law wouldn't get you. That's how you ended up here. The law decided when they got to the scene of the wreck that you just weren't running with your buddies right then. They think you must have stayed behind for some reason; but I'm going to surprise them when I deliver you to them as a present."

"Wow, what a brutal testimony of proof against me." He thought. "It's about like being slapped in the face with a bullwhip. So, that's why I was having, 'I'm going to kill you all' running through my mind when I woke up." The thought caused him to feel very bewildered. He just couldn't imagine himself as being that sort of a person, but she held the paper with the proof that said he was. What could have happened in his life he wondered, that could have made him turn out like that?

He tried not to let the way he was feeling inside show to the outside, but had to wait just a little bit to get his composure before he asked her. "You called me 'Turley' a while ago. Where did that come from?"

Toning down the conversation a bit seemed to have a favorable effect on the temperament of the girl, and she in turn spoke a little friendlier.

"Well, let's see." She said, and started scanning over the paper. "Down here it says that the other three guys were identified, but the one that ran with them that they called 'Turley' was not with them. So, that would be you, Turley."

She kind of made a cute little funny face, and asked, "What kind of name is that? Is that your last name? Surely no one would name their kid Turley as a first name."

"Well, like I said, I can't remember, so it is as strange to me as it is to you." He answered.

"Come on," She said, "You need to eat something, then, we need to get started. It will be too late to go this evening if we don't get started soon."

16

"Why are you concerned about whether I eat or not?" He asked. "If I'm the guy you say I am, why should you care?"

"I wouldn't want to make an animal go without eating, and to tell the truth, you look like you haven't eaten in days. You really look puny and gaunt, and I've heard that the food down at the jail is pretty sloppy. I may not be a good cook, but I think I can beat what I've heard they serve down there."

She began spooning the food to him, and added, "Besides, it's just the Christian thing to do. It is how I would want to be treated if I was in your place."

"Well, I hope you are feeling the Christian Spirit enough that if you have any sort of aspirin or something for a head ache, that you wouldn't mind sharing that with me." He said.

"Yes, I do, and pardon me. I brought it here for you and just forgot to give it to you. Here it is and here's some water."

She picked up the aspirin and gently put it to his lips to where he could take it in his mouth. Then she tipped the glass of water to his lips for him to take in the water to swallow the pill with. "I also bandaged up that cut on your head. That is a pretty good sized knot," She lightly touched his head where the knot was, and continued, "but the cut isn't bad enough to need stitches. Your head is probably hard enough that whatever it was that you butted with it got the worst end of the deal."

The conversation slowed down while she fed him the cereal. It tasted very good to him, and he wondered how long it had been since he had eaten.

"With what you said about the food in the jail, it doesn't really make me very anxious to get there." He said between bites.

"Actually," She said, "I am growing more reluctant to take you there. You really don't seem like the kind of guy that would do the things that you've done, and that is why I've got to really hurry and get it done. If I don't do it when I know it should be done, I'm afraid I could change my mind and start trying to believe that you aren't really who you are. That

could turn into a disaster, and I don't need any more disasters."

"Well, what if I'm not really who you think I am?" He said. "What if just by coincidence I happened to be someone who got robbed, and was left there where I was because they thought I was dead, and it just happened to be at the same time those hoodlums had the wreck on the bridge?"

She hesitated slightly before answering, but then said, "Well, the sheriff should be able to sort all that out, and find out who you are. I just have to do what I have to do in getting you out of here. I don't like having a strange man in my house."

"How did you get me in here anyway?" He asked. "You aren't a very big person. Did you have help?"

"I drug your nasty, bloody, muddy body in here." She said. "No, I didn't need any help. I've helped my grandpa around here enough that I know how to do things that other people struggle with, but not me.

"Now, we are going to get some clothes on you, so, I'm going to untie one arm, and help you put it through the shirt sleeve, then I'll tie your arm back up and untie the other arm, and get it through the sleeve, and tie it up again. If you try to make any wrong moves I'll whack you over the head, and put another big knot and cut on it; so you better behave yourself if you understand what's best for you."

He wondered where her grandpa was. It was evident that she was here alone, but he wondered if her husband and grandpa would be back sometime soon. He decided that they wouldn't be anytime this evening or she would probably wait for them before taking him in to the sheriff.

It was amazing to him how she carefully and very proficiently did every little detail of getting him back into clothes and ready to go in to the sheriff.

She stopped for a moment and gave him a funny look, and kind of shook her head. "I sure wasn't expecting you to be so cooperative. I figured you would be cussing me and threatening me, and all sorts of things. You do realize you may be on your way to prison, don't you?"

"Yeah," he answered, "I guess I'll deserve whatever I get, but, I'm hoping they will discover I'm not who you say I am, and I can find out just who I really am. I just don't feel like I am capable of doing all what the paper said those guys did. I just can't believe I would be part of that."

"Well, I had the duct tape ready to tape your mouth shut if you started cussing me, and threatening me. You may be just playing it cool, and have a plan to play on my sympathy and think I'll believe you are just an innocent victim, and change my mind about taking you to the sheriff, but I won't."

If she was surprised because of his actions, he thought, he was equally surprised by hers. Even though she thought he was a criminal, and deserved to be put in prison, she was treating him kind, and talking to him almost as if he was her friend. But still, she was very determined and firm in what she was doing.

Gently, but with no apologies she got him to put his arms through the shirt sleeves, and then tied him back up before she had him to put his legs into the pant-legs of his pants.

"That is a pretty bad bruise on your leg. You must have whacked it against something pretty hard to have it turn so blue like that." She said. Then she continued with the subject she had been talking about before.

"I've had experience with people who know all the right things to say to get people thinking the way they want them to." She said, "That's how my husband would do before he die.... before he did some of the things he would do."

He could tell she was frustrated with herself for letting it slip that her husband had died. She had tried to catch herself, but it had already happened. He thought that probably she had wanted him to think her husband could walk in anytime, and it would be sort of a safety thing for her.

"So, how did your husband die?" He asked.

"He was killed in a hunting accident last hunting season." she answered.

"Although, I'm not convinced it was an accident, but that is what it was called."

"Why? Was there someone who might have wanted him dead?"

"Well, a lot of this may be just speculation on my part, but, I think he was being used to try to get me to sell this property, and when it wasn't working out, I think he was sort of in the way, and a certain someone thought to get him out of the wayso that another method could be used to try to get me to sell."

"What about your grandpa?" Does he fit into the picture anywhere in this?"

"Look, I don't want to talk about this, and especially not to a total stranger, so let's just get on with the project at hand." She said, and continued getting ready to go to the pickup.

"Now, I'm going to leave your ankles and legs untied so that you can walk to the pickup, but I'm keeping a rope tied to one leg so that if you try to run or anything, I'll jerk your leg out from under you! Is that clear?"

"I won't be trying to do anything. I know you've got to do what you have to do. I really don't know any other way for me to find out who I am, and if I'm who you say I am, then I guess I need to face the music. It would be nice to find out that I'm not who you think I am, if I could be a different kind of person than that," He said.

He was struggling with the thought that he didn't want to go in to the sheriff, but decided that even if he was to get away from this girl, it wouldn't be long until he would be hunted down, and he still didn't have the strength to be running from the law.

She got him into the pickup, and tied the end of the rope tight to a bar of the seat frame under the seat. That would make it more difficult for him to suddenly get the door open and make a break. She seemed to have thought out each detail. It was evident that she was a smart lady.

She got in the pickup and put the key in and turned it to start the pickup. Nothing happened! "What is the matter with this crazy thing?" she asked.

She tried again. Still nothing happened! The starter didn't even click!

"Surely the battery isn't dead! I went to the mailbox yesterday and got the paper, and it was working just fine then!" She said.

She got out of the pickup and raised the hood. She looked to see if there was anything glaring out that she could notice.

The battery cables were fastened onto the battery good. She didn't know anything else to check that she would know anything about, but decided to turn on the lights and see if they were bright or dim. They were bright, so she determined that the battery wasn't dead.

"Well, we may as well go back into the house. Even if I knew what was the matter it would take too long to fix it and still get in to the sheriff's office today."

She untied the rope from under the seat, and they walked back to the house.

"Do you know anything about motors?" she asked.

"I don't know if I do or not." He said. "I was thinking when you were checking the battery that I could trace the wiring going to the starter and ignition and other places to see if a rat or a mouse has chewed the wiring in two. I guess I must know a few things about motors, but I don't remember where I learned it."

"I guess I'll let you do that tomorrow." She said. "Oh, this is terrible of me, asking you to fix the pickup so that I can take you to what may be your going to prison. I better watch you close. You may fix it where it will never run again if I let you get to working on it."

They went into the living room, and she helped him sit down on the couch.

"I'm sorry I don't have a television for you to watch." She said. "My grandpa didn't like them, and we never got one. I've heard people say that there is a lot of filth on them anyway nowadays, so I guess unless someone likes that sort of stuff a person isn't missing much.

"My grandpa was pretty old fashioned. He didn't even want a telephone."

He noticed that she said," My grandpa was pretty old fashioned." And that indicated to him that her grandpa was also dead.

She was busy in the kitchen, but she talked loud enough that he didn't have any trouble hearing her. "But, of course Grandpa and Grandma didn't have any other family after Mom and Dad got killed in a car accident, so we didn't have anyone to call anyway."

He remembered that she had said she didn't need any more disasters, and it sounded like she really did have quite a few. It suddenly occurred to him that this might be a very brave girl who was not really showing the heartache that she held inside. Outwardly she showed someone who carried on a normal everyday kind of life, but it sounded like there may be things that had happened in her life that could have destroyed someone who didn't have the fortitude she seemed to have.

He decided to casually ask a question that her answer would also answer the other question in his mind of whether her grandpa was still alive.

"So, how did your grandpa and grandma die?" he asked.

"Well, Grandma just kind of got old, and just died peacefully in her sleep, but Grandpa's death seemed like another suspicious happening to me." But then she must have realized that she had given information out that she hadn't intended to, and quickly added, "But, I'm rattling on, telling you things I don't have any business telling even a good

friend, and here you are a total stranger. I need to use a little more discretion. Grandpa said I was a blabbermouth, and I needed to not be talking so much."

"Well, tell me about this picture that I'm looking at here on the wall." He said.

The picture was a picture that was taken by a camera, and enlarged to an eight and a half by eleven picture of a place with a big rock right close in between two very steep hills, and very little space between the rock and one hill, and it looked like a very tight spot for a person to get stuck in between them. Written on the picture was, "BETWEEN A

ROCK AND A HARD PLACE." underneath that was the words, "When you are between a rock and a hard place, LOOK UP, and you just might find some help for your problem."

She walked into the living room wiping her hands on her apron, and said, "That is a picture Grandpa took of a place here on the ranch. He said he actually got hung up in that place one time. He said that he had often been in between a rock and a hard place, but never quite like that before." She kind of giggled a cute little laugh, and then added, "He said he looked up and there was a place on the rock that he could get a good grip, and pull himself up to where he could maneuver himself out of the situation. He thought that it was a good similarity to when we get in a situation that seems to be between a rock and a hard place, if we look up to God, we can find a way out of our dilemma."

"Your Grandpa sounds like a very smart man. Now, if I can change the subject for a moment; I've spent one night here in your house, and all day today, and now it looks like I'll be spending another night. You seem to know my name, but I don't know yours. Would it be alright if I ask you what your name is?"

"It's Kylie," she said. "I only know you by one name, so one name for me will be good enough."

"Thank you, Kylie, and I don't blame you even a little bit for keeping me tied up. Even though I know I would not do anything to hurt you, you don't know that, and you are right for not trusting me. But I want you to know I appreciate your kindness to me in the other ways you have shown a true Christian attitude."

"Well, I guess when I saw you so bloody and muddy and so weak that you couldn't help but fall face first into the puddle of fresh cow manure, I just had to take pity on you no matter what you have done in the past. I don't know if it is one of God's ways to humble you, or if there is some other reason things are working out like this; but I believe there is a reason for everything, and I believe God is working something out here."

"Well," Turley said, "that brings to mind something I heard somewhere; that everything happens for a reason, and sometimes the reason is that we have done something stupid. And since for every action there is a reaction, the reaction for our stupid action is that we have got ourselves into a lot of trouble. I hope the reason that I am having these things happen to me is not because I have done something very stupid."

Kylie continued working in the kitchen, and soon there was a delightful aroma of something cooking drifting into the living room.

"Turley, do you like fried chicken?" Kylie called from the kitchen.

"If whatever you are fixing tastes as good as it smells, then I'm sure that no matter what it is, I'll like it just fine," Turley answered.

Turley, as he was known to Kylie, had discovered that Kylie had not tied him back up as tightly after he had put his clothes back on as he had been earlier. He was very uncomfortable being tied up, and when he found he could loosen the ropes just a little bit it was a lot easier to put up with. As he worked with them more he felt that he could possibly even free himself from the ropes. He decided that after she had fed him and gone to bed it might be that he could free himself and slip out in the night. He really didn't want to go to the sheriff like this. He hoped that something would jog his memory and he would remember who he really was, and if he was really this Turley guy, then he would rather turn himself in than to be taken in by someone else. There might be a possibility that if he turned himself in the court would go easier on him.

The more he worked on the ropes, the more he felt that he would be able to get himself free, so he decided to make it look like he was still tied up until after Kylie had gone to bed.

Kylie nearly had the food ready to eat when someone knocked on the door.

"Who in the world could that be and why are they knocking on the back door?" Kylie said. "No one ever comes way out here. They didn't even when Grandpa was still alive."

Kylie opened the door, and the man didn't wait to be invited in, he just pushed his way on into the house. Kylie, screamed and backed away from him, but he calmly said, "That's okay little lady, this is a friendly visit. I just didn't think you would let me in when you saw who I was."

"I certainly would not have," Kylie said. "And I would appreciate it if you would just turn around and leave right now."

"Oh, that's not going to happen." the man said. "I'm here to buy your property, and I'm going to make you an offer that you just can't refuse."

"Oh you think I can't refuse, do you?" Kylie was angry now. "Well, I refuse to even listen to your offer. This property is not for sale at any price. But if I was to sell it, it would not be for sale to you. Now get out!"

Turley could hear every word from the other room, and now he worked franticly to get loose from the ropes. He was glad that he had continued working to loose them, and now he was almost free.

The man had a devious smile on his face as he came toward Kylie. "Look little lady, I know you have been having problems one right after another. First your grandfather was found dead out on your ranch, and there have been no clues turn up to explain what happened to him. Then the majority of your cattle turn up missing, and things are not working out for you in finding out what happened to them. Before you can recover from that loss your husband accidentally shoots himself while trying to get through a fence last hunting season."

The man was slowly moving toward Kylie as he was talking. "You certainly would want this all to stop, but I can guarantee that it is only going to get worse.

"You are a smart woman, you can figure a lot of things out, and you have been managing so far; but you know that you won't be able to keep going if things keep happening like they have been. What you need to do is to let me take this worthless ranch off your hands, and you would have enough money to move into town and find you a job where you wouldn't have to work so hard." He started reaching out for her, and said, "Come on now, let's sit down and talk about this."

"Just stay away from me!!" Kylie was saying as she backed away from the man. She backed over beside the counter in the kitchen and reached for an iron skillet that was sitting there. The man lunged forward and grabbed her wrist before she could swing the skillet at him. Then he whirled her around till he was standing behind her, and was holding her around her waist with one hand and he twisted the skillet from her with his other hand.

"You are a little bit feisty for such a sweet little thing," The man said. "But you just aren't any match for a big strong man like me."

The man nuzzled the back of Kylie's neck, and nibbled on her ear.

Kylie screamed, and fought back as best she could, but the man was right, she was no match for him since he was so much bigger and stronger than she was.

The man was laughing with an anxious sort of attitude, as though he was anticipating something, and could hardly wait for it to happen.

"I know a sweet little thing like you gets lonely here all by yourself since your husband died. Why don't you just calm down now, and let me keep you company for a while, and you will feel a lot better, don't you think?"

The man suddenly felt the barrel of a rifle behind his right ear, and heard Turley say, "I believe the lady has let it be known that she does not want your company, and doesn't even want you in her house. Do you want to walk out that door now, or should we carry you out?"

"Who are you, where did you come from?" The man asked.

"We aren't going to have a question and answer session at this time." Turley said, "We may have one later, but you will be the one to answer the questions at that time."

The man kind of backed and walked sideways to the door sort of motioning for Turley to not point the gun at him; almost tripping on a chair, then went through the door in a hurry, and was gone.

Turley let the barrel of the rifle drop to where it was pointing toward the floor, and Kylie rushed to him with tears in her eyes, and hugged him and kissed him on the cheek.

Turley felt a sweet rush of emotion go through him.

Kylie was shaking, and almost crying. "How did you know where the gun was?"

"You brought it into the living room earlier and I was watching and saw where you put it."

"I had you tied up, how did you get loose?"

"Oh, sometimes a person can do a lot of seemingly impossible things if it becomes necessary." Turley said.

CHAPTER THREE: I didn't take your money

Kylie was still quite shaken, but soon regained her composure and went about getting the rest of the meal ready for them to eat.

"Now see what you've done for yourself." She said. "You don't get to have me feed you now. You'll have to feed yourself tonight."

"Yeah, what a bummer," Turley affirmed "I try to help you out, and that's what I get for it. I was enjoying being fed. I can't remember the last time I got fed by a pretty lady." Kylie sort of blushed, and Turley continued, "Actually. I can't remember the last time I fed myself even." A serious look came over his face, and he said, "I wish something would

happen, or that I would see something or do something that would jog my memory to where I could remember things."

They were sitting down now, and Kylie reached over and put her hand on Turley's knee. "I really did think that you were making that up about not being able to remember, but I think I'm starting to believe you now." She patted his knee and continued, "It must be awful not being able to remember who you are. If you were in on that robbery, you were a

different person then than you are now. Whatever happened that led you to the place that you would do something like that turned you into that person; but this is who you really are; the person I see right here with me now."

They sat at the table together side by side, and Kylie thought, "This seems so right. This seems more like I wanted it to be with my husband Carl."

Suddenly Kylie said, "Wait. We were about to start eating, but earlier you said something about asking for a blessing on your food before you started eating. Did you really mean that?"

"Of course I did, and I didn't intend to start eating now before I asked for a blessing on the food, and thanked God for it." Turley said.

"Would you do it out loud for both of us?" Kylie asked.

"Of course; I was just going to ask you if it would be alright for me to do that."

Kylie listened to Turley's prayer, and she could tell that it was not a put on prayer by someone who was not familiar with praying. When he had finished and said "amen" Kylie said, "And I would like to add to this prayer; Dear God, please guide us in what we do about finding out

who Turley really is, and if he really is who it appears that he is, then help things to work out for him, and be with him through it all, amen."

Turley reached over and put his hand on Kylie's cheek.

"Thank you Kylie; you are a very sweet person." Kylie reached up and put her hand on Turley's hand and brought it around to her mouth and kissed his hand. "I'm beginning to understand that you are too Turley, or whatever your name is. It is getting harder and harder to believe that you are one of those who were in that robbery."

"I think I remember you saying something about you may not be a good cook. Well, if you aren't then you sure accidentally did everything just right on everything you cooked here. I can't remember ever having a meal as good as this one." Turley said.

32

"Well, if what you have been telling me is true, you probably can't remember ever eating any meal." Kylie answered. "So, of course this would be the best meal you ever remember eating."

"Well yes, that is true, but I certainly can't imagine that I ever had a meal that tasted as good as this one does. This is wonderful."

"Well, you are probably just trying to be kind, but thank you Turley for the compliment."

After eating Turley helped with doing the dishes, and then they went to the living room to discuss the plans for the next day.

"If I can find out what the problem is with the pickup tomorrow I suppose we should go ahead and go talk to the sheriff, but I would like to be the one who is turning myself in.

It might possibly go easier on me if I did." Turley looked at Kylie to see what her reaction would be. "I seriously doubt there would be any reward for a two bit criminal like me if I was one of them in on the robbery. Of course it may not go any easier on me if I turn myself in either though, so if you would like to get the credit for turning me in, that would be alright too."

"Let's just take one thing at a time." Kylie said, "I don't know if I want to turn you in now or not." Kylie looked as if she might start crying. "Maybe we could wait for a while, and maybe you will get your memory back. You may not have had anything to do with it." After saying that, she had a more cheerful look on her face. "We may find out that you aren't

Mr. Turley at all. You may be someone with a nice name."

"Well, if Turley is the last name it would be alright, but I don't know how Turley is for a first name. I guess it would be alright if that is what someone wants to name their kid." Turley said. "But, I'll bet it would end up being changed to 'Turkey' by the kids at school."

Kylie laughed. "Are you sure that isn't what happened to you, so you know for sure it would happen? Maybe you are getting your memory back."

Kylie didn't wait for an answer, she continued, "Okay Turkey, if it is alright with you we can just start out by seeing what can be done with the pickup, and play it by ear from then on."

Turkey, as Kylie's new name for him would be, said, "That sounds good to me. I'm pretty much like the picture your grandpa took. I'm in between a rock and a hard place, so this is a good time to 'LOOK UP' to the Lord, and let Him work things out from here on."

"If you can stay around long enough, I'll take you and show you where that place is on the ranch. When you go and see it you will see why someone would want to try to get through there instead of going a long way around, but once someone gets started they can find themselves kind of stuck unless they have been there before and know how to keep from it."

Turkey nodded to Kylie, and said, "I would love to see it. I hope if we go to the sheriff's tomorrow that I don't get thrown in the slammer. How far away is it? Maybe we could go see it before we go to the sheriff?"

"Now wait a minute," Kylie said, "I thought we decided for you to wait a while and see if maybe your memory could get jogged and you could remember who you are. I was going to put you to work as my new hired hand, except the pay might be lower than you would agree to."

"Well, I'm already indebted to you for what you've done for me, so I need to work quite a while to just get started out even. You could start me out paying me nothing, and then if I work out to be a good hand, after a while you could double my wages."

Kylie laughed, and he thought she had a real cute and sweet laugh. He realized that he was going to have to be on guard all the time, because since he could not remember any of his past, he didn't know if he was married or not. He certainly didn't want to let himself get to caring for this girl, and then find that he was married. That could be a heartbreak just waiting to happen. And even if he wasn't married, if it turned out that he was this Turley fellow, and was in with the others on the robbery he would be going to jail anyway.

Turkey was a little bit puzzled that Kylie didn't say more about the man who had pushed himself into the house and had made her get so upset. She seemed hesitant to talk about quite a few things, so he decided that if she wanted to talk about it she would, and if she didn't want to talk about it he didn't want to pry. But then again maybe she was waiting for him to ask her about it. He decided to casually bring the subject up and see where it went from there.

"That old boy had a lot of nerve just coming into the house uninvited like he did, didn't he?"

Kylie looked up, then looked back down, and waited just a little before she answered. "Yes, he is really an obnoxious person. He has all kinds of money, and thinks he can have anything he decides he wants. He is as slinky as a snake in the way he does things. His ego is as big as a mountain.

"He offered Grandpa a pretty sizeable amount for the ranch, but

Grandpa said he didn't want to sell. That made him mad, and he has been determined that he was going to have this ranch one way or another."

She put her hand to her face, and Turkey could see she was about to cry. She turned away to keep him from seeing, but he had already noticed,

"He paid Carl to court me and marry me so that Carl could work on me to sell the ranch, because he owns all the property around it, and he is just greedy enough that he feels like he has to have it all regardless of who it hurts or what damage to lives it would cause.

"I really believed that Carl loved me, and I thought he would be a great help to Grandpa in running the ranch, but I found out he was working against us at every turn. I wish I had listened to Grandpa when he kept telling me that Carl was not right for me."

Turkey went to Kylie and put his arms around her. She sobbed a little bit, but then pushed him away and said, "This is no way for me to act. Grandpa told me I have to be strong when times get rough or the enemy will take advantage of my weakness."

"Well, from what I heard the intruder say, things are really, really getting rough for you, and it sounded like he was threatening to keep making them even get rougher if you didn't sell. I would like to help you stop him if there is anything I can do."

Kylie turned and looked straight at Turkey. "Well, I don't intend to be taken in again, so I've got to make sure you are not another of Brackley's hired men who is going to lure me into thinking he is on my side, and then turn out like Carl did, and be a thorn in my side."

"I could never do something like that." Turkey said.

"Well, I've got to be sure before I could trust you. This is quite a story you are telling me about losing your memory, and I just wonder a lot about you forgetting who you are, but you sure didn't forget who God is. There are so many things that you can remember, but then some of the things that you say you can't remember makes me wonder if you have a

selective memory of what is convenient and what is not convenient to go along with what you might have planned."

"Well, it's not like my whole brain got fried," Turkey said. "I don't know why I can remember some things, and can't remember other things. I guess some things have been instilled into my brain so well that it is like a second nature to me. I remembered all about cars, and rivers, and people and all things like that, but I just can't remember who I am."

"Well, I want so much to trust you, but you almost are too good to be true. You seem to always say just what I would want you to say, and do just what I would want you to do. That is just how Carl did at first, because Brackley had coached him and trained him, and then sent him to me to try to get the property away from me and Grandpa."

Suddenly a smile came over Kylie's face. "Grandpa never quit trying to get Carl to trust in the Lord." She said. "He kept pointing to the picture he titled 'Between a Rock and a Hard Place' and told him that if he ever got down on his luck and could bring himself to trust the Lord, all he had to do was to look up, and he could find an answer to many problems."

Kylie's eyes filled with tears, and she said, "Carl caused Grandpa to lose his faith in me a lot, because he thought I was standing with Carl against him, but I never was. He could see what Carl was like on the inside, and he thought I was going that way too. Carl thought Grandpa was just an old fashioned person who was living in a different age than what we are in. He even thought Grandpa had a lot of money hid some where on the ranch, because Grandpa never used banks or credit cards. He only used cash all the time."

There was silence for a while. Turkey didn't know what to say right then, but soon Kylie spoke again. "If Grandpa did have some money hid somewhere, it would have been nice if he had given me some clue as to where he hid it. With nearly all the cattle gone, it would be nice to be able to restock the ranch. I know I'll never get any word about who rustled them. The law around here just doesn't do much for people like me."

"How have you been able to keep the ranch going with your grandpa and your husband gone?" Turkey asked.

"Well, it hasn't been hard to keep it going, because it is very much in the red, and is going down the drain right now, and it doesn't take much to keep it going like that," Kylie said. "But I've got to get it going back in the black again somehow. But, unless I can get some money somewhere, I don't know just what to do. I sure hate the thought of taking

out a mortgage. Brackley would love for me to borrow the money I would need, and then he would make sure someway that I was not able to pay it back."

Turkey raised his eyes and looked at Kylie, then said,

"Well, I sure wish I had some money to give you, but somehow I came up short of a billfold and anything else I may have had in my pockets, so I don't know if I even had any money before or not."

"Well, I certainly didn't take your billfold or anything. You didn't have anything in your pockets when I took your clothes to wash them. Kylie said,

"Oh, no, I didn't mean to sound like I thought you did. I had already checked to see if I had any identification on me, and I didn't have anything in any of my pockets. Someone had cleaned me out before I woke up."

"I wouldn't take your money anyway.' Kylie said.

"But, what I asked about keeping the ranch going was: there is an awfully lot of work to run a ranch, and without your husband and grandpa; how is all the work that needs to be done taken care of?"

"Granddad had everything really fixed up so that one person could do most everything most of the time. He has some of the other ranchers lined up to help with rounding up the calves and the branding and vaccination and ear-marking and all the other. They would help him, and then he would help them with their cattle. We feed alfalfa pellets to the cattle in the wintertime along with hay, and one person can do that because we only run about three hundred head of cattle. We feed the big round bales of hay. Then of course we have to go around and break the ice in the winter so that the cattle can get water, and all the fences need to be kept up."

Turkey seemed to be able to get a good picture in his mind of all this, and wondered why it seemed familiar to him. It was as if he almost remembered doing it himself, but he just couldn't get his memory to kick in.

"I think I could enjoy doing work like that" Turkey said.

"But that Brackley feller is not going to keep quiet about me being here, so if the law is looking for me, they will no doubt be paying you a visit. I may not get to stay around long enough to be of any help to you."

CHAPTER FOUR: Between a rock and a hard place

Kylie was yawning and said that she thought it was bedtime. "Am I going to have to tie you up again tonight to keep you from slipping off into the night, or will you still be here in the morning?" she asked.

"I'll still be here in the morning, but should I go out and sleep in the barn?"`

"No, you can sleep in the same bedroom you slept in last night. The bathroom is down the hall and the second door on the right; but then I guess I told you that earlier, so you already knew that." She threw him a pair of her husband's pajamas, and said, "I'll get up about six in the morning and get started with some breakfast."

Kylie had felt sleepy before she went to bed, but now she was wide awake. She had started thinking about the things that had happened recently and now all she could do is lie there in bed thinking.

It was strange she thought that this man, whoever he was, was so different than the type of person he appeared to be. He appeared to be someone who didn't care about how he looked; he was unshaven, needed a haircut, and just looked pretty scrubby. His appearance certainly didn't seem to reflect his personality. He acted polite and like a gentleman, and seemed to want to please in every way he could. He didn't seem to have the attitude that he didn't care what people thought of the way he looked, he just looked like he didn't care. When he talked he made you feel important as though you were the only thing that mattered right then. And when you talked he listened as though what you were saying was the most important thing that could be said.

It was rather disturbing to her to think about the feelings she was beginning to have. At first the only thing she wanted to do was get him out of her house, but now she found herself enjoying having him around. She was beginning to feel comfortable around him, and she wasn't sure that was a good thing. She even found herself comparing the comfort she felt

around him to the way she had felt about her husband Carl.

How she regretted being so rebellious against what her grandfather had told her about what he saw in Carl. She felt so sure that her grandfather was wrong, and that he would soon find out that he was wrong. But, one by one everything her grandfather had pointed out proved to be right, and Carl was soon treating her as though she was his servant instead of his wife. He didn't turn out to be the help to her grandfather that she thought he would, and didn't seem to have any desire to learn about ranching. He was more interested in going to town and gambling away the money that was designated to other things.

One thing that tormented her, and brought tears every time she thought about it was that very soon after Carl learned that her grandfather had put her name on the deed to the ranch as co-owner and would be full owner if anything happened to her grandfather, something did happen to him.

When he didn't come home one day, but his horse came home without him, the other ranchers got together and searched over the ranch, and found him supposedly having been thrown from his horse and killed. Kylie just couldn't make herself believe that could happen to her grandpa. He was just too good with horses for that to happen, as far as she could believe. But what could she do? The investigation concluded that was what happened, so that is how it stood.

Carl just wouldn't let up after that in trying to get her to sell the ranch. She was glad that she had that stubbornness in her that her grandpa was always talking about when she made up her mind about something. She knew that if she sold the ranch Carl would take the money and run, and she wouldn't ever see any of it, or ever see him again.

Kylie felt that Carl knew something about so many of the cattle being rustled, and probably was in on it some way. It was probably another thing he thought would convince her to sell, because now there would be no money from selling the calves. She felt that he probably got quite a bit of money out of the deal some way, or maybe was promised a lot of money; but what happened to him later may have been a way to get out of giving him the money, and possibly be sure he didn't tell anyone what really happened to the cattle. But she had no proof. She was convinced that none of the dreams she had once had about her and Carl would ever come true; but had instead pretty much turned into a nightmare. She had decided to divorce him.

But evidently the person Carl was working for in trying to get her to sell the ranch grew impatient with Carl and decided to use other methods to try to get her to sell.

So, now this stranger shows up. Is he part of the plan to get her to sell the ranch? This would be a very dramatic way to enter into the picture if he is.

No, that would be impossible to stage everything to happen the way it did. When Turkey arrived at the ranch the way he did it was definitely not play acting. But, just not knowing anything about him was definitely something to cause her to watch closely for any insincere actions on his part. She decided she would be very cautious and stay very

alert in her dealings with this man. If he was just working on gaining her trust, then it was working. She was nearly worn down to where she was ready to believe anything that seemed to be an answer to her problems. She realized that she was already starting to compare this stranger that she didn't even know his name to her late husband. She acknowledged to herself that she had even noticed that he wasn't wearing a wedding ring; although she could tell that he had worn one quite recently, because the skin on his ring finger was lighter where a ring had once been.

"This is crazy," she thought, "I'm like some boy crazy school girl. I guess I've just been out here alone so long that now I start looking at the first man that comes along as a potential boy friend."

She was slightly embarrassed when she remembered about feeling so comfortable just having him around, and comparing that to how she had come to feel uncomfortable around her husband Carl.

"I can't start thinking this way," she thought, "This is just an echo of my dreams that I had for me and Carl. I have nothing to build another dream on.

"I have just been sheltered so much all my life, even though Grandpa and Grandma taught me so many things about how some people are underhanded in their dealings, and will do nearly anything to deceive, I just didn't really get the true picture. But I am seeing it now."

Kylie felt a surge of distress flow through her, and she rolled over and pounded her pillow. Then she remembered what her grandpa would tell her to do when she felt distraught. "Just cool it Kylie. Getting distraught will not solve anything; it will only give you gray hair, and you will still have your problem. Take your troubles to The Lord, and He will give you guidance in what you should do." He would say.

Then she remembered something else her grandpa had said. "One way God uses to talk to us is to remind us of something by causing us to think of it. Sometimes it may be scriptures that can be applied as an answer to our problems, or sometimes it might be advice we had received on some problem at another time that will also apply to the particular problem we have at the time."

"So," Kylie thought, "God is offering to help me if I just turn to Him."

Kylie prayed, and cried, and told God all about the way she was feeling, and thanked Him for being there to give her guidance. When she finished she felt like a great load had been lifted off her shoulders.

Now Kylie had exhausted herself with all she had to think about, and slowly faded into a peaceful sleep.

The night passed, but not with peaceful dreams for Turkey. He would dream a dream, and wake up, and each time he would try to analyze the dream to see if he could pull some resemblance out of it that would point him to his real life. He dreamed of fire, and then dreamed of wrestling with several men all at the same time, and it seemed that every one of them was trying to keep him from going somewhere that he wanted to go. He kept dreaming all sorts of dreams that he couldn't make any sense out of. He wished that he could just sleep without dreaming anything unless his dreams could be about something that would point him to how his real life was.

While trying to analyze his dreams his thoughts wandered to where he began thinking of the things that had happened recently. It was frightening to think about losing his memory and all. What was his life really like? Was he really this Turley character? Is that the kind of life he was living?

There would have been no doubt in his mind that he was not him if it hadn't been for the words that were going through his mind when he woke up by the river. The words that the paper said one of the men robbing the place had said to the people that were being robbed; that he was going to kill all of them. The very words that he could hear in his mind as though it was him saying them.

It was bewildering to him to find that he was unable to remember his past, but then to discover that he may be a criminal was so much more disturbing. He just didn't feel that he had the type of character that would lean in that direction.

The evidence seemed to prove that his feeling was wrong however. The evidence seemed to prove that he was at least with them, whether he was in on the robbery, or had just been taken hostage, but he just couldn't shake the way the words kept coming to him as though it was him saying them, and not as though he was just repeating what he had heard someone else say.

His troubled thoughts swarmed through his mind, and for quite some time they barricaded sleep from finding him, but sometime during the night a restless sort of sleep subdued his thoughts and he was able to sleep a short while.

Finally morning came, and he awoke hearing faint sounds of Kylie in the kitchen, and could smell coffee in the making.

He pulled on his clothes and went into the bathroom. When he looked in the mirror he could see what Kylie meant about him looking like he hadn't eaten in a long time. Besides needing a shave, he looked gaunt and haggard. "Who am I?" he asked himself.

Kylie had heard him close the bathroom door and she knocked on the door and said, "There are some combs and razors in the drawers. Help yourself to any of the aftershave and stuff that my husband had."

"Thanks." Turkey said and pulled open a drawer.

He did the best he could with his hair, but wondered how long it had been since he had got a haircut. He liked his looks a lot better after he had shaved. By now the smell of breakfast was luring him to the kitchen.

When he saw Kylie going about the kitchen he had to just stop and get a good look at her. She looked so beautiful. "She looks just like an angel." He thought. "Well, she is an angel. God had her there to look out for me when I needed help."

"You sure look nice, and breakfast sure smells good." He said as she handed him a cup of coffee."

She turned and smiled up at him. "You look a lot better with a shave, but I'm going to cut a bunch of that hair off of you, and then you will look even better.

"You'll have to add whatever to your coffee to fix it the way you like it." She added. "The sugar and cream are on the table."

As they finished breakfast Kylie said, "I need to ride out and look at some fence that I have been meaning to check; I may have to do a little bit of mending on it, but it shouldn't take much. If you'd like to ride out with me we could swing by and look at 'Between a Rock and a Hard Place.'"

"Sounds like a plan." Turkey said, so after they finished the dishes Kylie handed Turkey a cowboy hat and said "Try that on. If it will fit, it will keep the sun out of your eyes."

Turkey tried it on and said, "It fits perfect." So they went out and saddled up two horses.

"I didn't know if you rode horses or not." Kylie said.

"Well, if you had asked me if I did, I wouldn't have known what to answer." Turkey said, "But I guess we are about to find out."

"Well, that sure wasn't the first time you ever saddled a horse," Kylie said, "The way you move sure indicates to me that you have had at least a little bit of experience around a ranch. It is a little too soon to feel real sure about it, but if that is true, then you may be in the right place for something to happen to jog your memory."

They mounted up, and after they had ridden for a while Kylie said, "Nice. You ride like an old hand. You may work out as a ranch hand alright if you can stay out of jail."

"I guess we'll see what happens. Never can tell what a day will bring."

"That's for sure." Kylie answered. "Two days ago if someone had told me I would be riding out to check fence with a total stranger today like I am, I would have thought they had lost their mind. But now, I'm not sure I haven't lost my mind for the things I have done in the last two days. This is so out of character for me."

"Well, I think that the things you have done in the last two days are very admirable. You sure came to my rescue, and I don't blame you one bit for being cautious about it. If I am who it looks like I am, then even I don't know how I'll be if or when my memory comes back."

"Have there been any times that you thought maybe you were remembering anything at all?" Kylie asked.

"I've been having weird dreams the last couple nights, and I thought maybe I would dream dreams that would involve something about how my life went, but so far my dreams have been so weird I sure couldn't get any clues from them. I am hoping that I still have memory in my subconscious mind, and I thought that if I dreamed about things that happened to me, and then if I remembered my dreams it might jog my

memory."

"Cool," Kylie said, "I sure hope it works."

Kylie was a beautiful sight as she rode along Turkey thought. She really looked nice in her blue jeans and shirt, and her cowgirl hat and boots, and riding along on her horse as though she was part of it. Turkey thought that this would make a beautiful picture if he had a camera. But, since he didn't have a camera, he would burn that picture into his mind so that he would not forget it.

The sky above, the puffy white clouds, the open range all somehow reached far down into the soul of Turkey, and was calling back memories of a different time and place. But as hard as he tried, he just could not hold on to the feelings long enough to remember when or where it was. Looking across the land gave him a peaceful feeling even at the same time he had a desperate feeling of trying to pull it all together to identify the memories that were trying to break through.

Finally he decided he just had to not let it get to him, and he would just enjoy the ride, and the time he got to spend with Kylie.

Kylie reigned in her horse and turned it to the left of how they had been going. "I see a young heifer that I've been a little concerned about." She said. "When I was putting the bulls in with the cows so the cows would be bred, I somehow let her get mixed in with the older cows. I didn't intend for her to get bred yet being as young as she is, but she had different ideas about that I guess, so now I'm wondering how it's going to be when it comes time for her to have her calf."

Kylie nudged her horse forward and rode toward where she saw the heifer. Turkey followed on his horse.

The heifer was lying down, and as soon as Kylie dismounted she opened her saddle bag and pulled out a small short silver chain with the links twisted and made so they would lie flat, and a come along. Turkey instantly saw what she was going to do. The young heifer had started having her calf, but it was too large to be born easily, and Kylie was going to pull the calf so that it wouldn't die before being born.

"It is quite fortunate that we rode out today," Kylie said, "This is happening much sooner than I thought it would." She fastened the small chain around the front legs of the calf that were all that was showing, and Turkey helped her work the cable of the come along out far enough to connect it to the lower part of a big bush. Then Kylie began working the come along. Turkey watched as the calf slowly entered the outside world. The new mother cow seemed very relieved to have all this over with, and seemed quite proud of her new baby calf.

Kylie looked at Turkey and said, "I've had to pull a lot of calves without the come along, but it is much easier this way."

"I'm very impressed," Turkey said, "You are a number one grade A rancher Miss Kylie, and I know I must have done this kind of work at some time in my life, because I knew just what you were going to do, and it was just what I would have done if I had come across a situation like this."

"That is very good." Kylie said as she cleaned her hands, first with paper towel, and then with a packet of moist towel wipes that she also had in her saddle bag, "So you won't need so much training while becoming my new ranch hand."

They rode on to the place where Kylie wanted to check the fence, and it did need a little bit of mending. Turkey helped her stretch the fence wires back up where it needed it, and Kylie said, "Well, I am impressed with your expertise in fixing fence. You evidently have done quite a lot of mending fence at some time in your life. Some of the things you knew are not things that a person just automatically knows without having the experience."

"Well, I did feel right at home, where ever that home might have been. I think that if there is anything that can happen to jog my memory, it could very well be something that happens on this ranch."

A soft breeze whispered to them as they sat on a log and ate a sandwich and drank some tea that Kylie had prepared for them, then they rode on over to the place that had been named, "Between a Rock and a Hard Place."

It was even more interesting than Turkey had thought it would be. It was right where a person would probably choose to go in order to get to a beautiful meadow just beyond it, but would prove to be a tight squeeze to get through it. A person would have to go through it, or climb up a steep bank to get over it, or go quite a distance around. The hill came down steep on one side, and met a big rock so close that it left only a little space to get through if someone chose to try to go through that way. Then a very steep hill on the other side joined the rock, leaving only a very narrow opening between the two steep hills.

Turkey dismounted and said, "I'd like to look this over a bit."

Kylie Said, "Go right ahead, I'll be right back." and she rode on down another trail.

Turkey walked over and purposely squeezed between the rock and the hard place. "Now Lord, I am in between a rock and a hard place, and I am going to look up to you, and trust you to help me with my problems. I am at peace about all this, because when I prayed about it when I first woke up and couldn't remember who I was, it was like you spoke to me and said, "Just keep cool, I've got this." I trust you, because when it is in your hands, I know it will be handled right. Also Father, I pray that you will help Kylie with all the problems she has. Amen"

Turkey opened his eyes and looked up. There he saw the place where Kylie's grandfather said was a good place to get a hand hold to pull up and help get out from between the rock and a hard place. He reached up and got a good grip, and pulled himself up. He was about to swing over and get free from the place when he saw something else that he thought was curious. He pulled himself up higher and could see that there was an opening in the rock up above. It wasn't anything that he would ordinarily be curious about, but this time he just felt drawn to it. He pulled himself up even higher, and could see that it had dirt and dried grass put in the pocket like opening. Most people would probably not think anything about it, and he probably wouldn't normally, but this time he dug into the dirt and began digging it out. After quite a lot of dirt had been pulled out, he felt some sort of metal box. He dug out more dirt and then worked the metal box loose and pulled it out. When he opened the lid he found something wrapped in brown paper bags. There was a note just inside the first bag.

To whoever finds this money: This money is for whoever finds it, because I was going to give it to my grand daughter, but I don't trust her husband. I would like for her to have it, but not him. I hope she is the one who finds it, but I hope she is not still with him when she does. I am just praying that God will help the right person to find it.

Turkey put the money back in the little steel box and slid it back into the pocket of the rock. Kylie was just getting back.

"Come here Kylie." Turkey called. Kylie dismounted and came on over.

"Go ahead and get in there and before you look up, pray that God will give you answers to your problems. I did, and I feel one hundred percent better than I did before."

Kylie was somewhat puzzled at Turkey's attitude, because he seemed exited and happy in a way that he hadn't been in all the time she had known him. She entered the tight squeeze and then said a prayer. She opened her eyes and looked up.

"I can see the hand grip place Grandpa told about, but I don't think I'm tall enough to reach it." Kylie said.

"You are small enough that you wouldn't get stuck in there anyway." Turkey said, "But there is something else I want you to see, so come on out, and I'll get in there and then I'll lift you up to where you can see it."

Kylie was more puzzled now, but came back out and let Turkey get in. It was a little bit difficult to get Kylie where he could lift her up to see into the small pocket in the rock. "Can you see the little hole in the rock up there?" Turkey asked.

"Yes, I can, and it looks like there is some sort of little box in there." Kylie answered.

"There is. Pull it out, and just wait till you see what is in it."

Kylie tugged the box out of the hole and Turkey lowered her back down, and then squeezed out of the tight spot.

Kylie was getting more excited now, and anxiously opened the lid of the box. "I can hardly believe this." She said as she read the note. "I'm just overwhelmed at this."

"It looks like you will be able to restock with cattle now." Turkey was smiling.

Kylie had tears in her eyes, but she was smiling too.

Kylie opened one of the paper bags of money. "Look at this; these bills are all big bills, and look how many of them.

There is no telling how long he was saving this money up. It had to be for an awfully long time."

Kylie looked up at Turkey and slowly shook her head.

"When you found this money you could have just never ever have let me know about it, and then you could have come back later and got it, and had it all for yourself."

"That wouldn't have been right. It's your money. I couldn't do something like that." Turkey said.

"Well, if you were in on that robbery with those other guys you could have, and probably would have. I don't think you were with them."

Turkey was glad at this point that he hadn't told her about how he had the words, "I'm going to kill you, I'm going to kill all of you" going through his mind when he woke up; and it was as if he had been saying them. If she knew about that she would not be so convinced that he was not with them, just as he was not convinced. For the time being he felt like it was important that she trust him. He hoped that his memory would kick in soon, and he would have some answers to the mystery. The biggest mystery to him about it was that if he was with them and was in on the robberies, why would he feel so against that sort of behavior now just because he had lost his memory.

Kylie interrupted his thoughts by saying, "Well, half of this is yours, because you found it."

"Oh, no, I couldn't do that either. It is all yours. Your grandpa wanted you to have it, and he would have just given it to you if it hadn't been for your husband being the way he was. He probably intended to give you some sort of hint about where to find it, and actually did with the picture, telling you to look up when you got in between a rock and a

hard place; meaning this place here; but died before he found any other way to make it plainer. He just felt like there was more of a chance of you getting it this way than if he had given it to you when Carl was around, because you wouldn't have had it long anyway if he had given it to you then."

"You are certainly right about that." Kylie agreed. "He would have lost it all gambling in no time."

"Do you think we ought to get back and let me get started checking the pickup out? There's no telling when you might need it, and it would be better if I can get it going so that it will be ready when you do."

55

"You're right," Kylie said, "I just got so excited about your find here that I forgot about everything else."

"This box may be difficult to get back to the house with." Kylie said. "A least it is going to be hard to get up in the saddle with it."

"You go ahead and get in the saddle, then I'll hand it up to you. Then if you want you can hand it back to me after I get mounted, and I think I'll be able to carry it without it being too much trouble. It doesn't seem like such a big box until thinking about trying to carry it while riding a horse." Turkey commented.

"I wonder how Granddad got it out here." Kylie said. "But then I shouldn't wonder. He was always very good at figuring ways to do things."

They rode back to the ranch house and Kylie insisted on getting something to eat before Turkey started on the pickup.

"You'll only have time to get your hands real dirty, and then you will spend more time having to clean up than you would gain by starting first."

"You are a smart girl." Turkey said, "I don't know if I would have thought of that or not. Is there anything I can do to help you?"

"No, but it is about time for the news and weather to come on. I don't have a TV, but there is a radio in the living room, if you would like to listen. I can hear it in the kitchen while I get us something to eat."

Turkey found the radio and turned it on just as they announced that it was time for the news and weather.

"I knew it! I knew it!" Kylie almost shouted as she came running into the living room. "I knew you weren't one of those guys that were doing all the robberies!"

It had just come over the radio that they had apprehended the fourth man involved in the robberies that the other three that had been in the wreck on the bridge had done. In more detail they explained that he was called "Turley" because it was a nickname he had been called since he was a child when he had asked his dad if he had 'turly' hair, because he was unable to pronounce "curly" with a 'C'.

The news anchor also explained why he had not been with them in the wreck. It seems that someone had been able to get to a phone and call the police, and Turley was in the getaway car waiting for the others to complete the robbery.

When they came out he would have the car ready to make the getaway. But, when Turley realized that the police were arriving before the others completed the robbery, he decided to save his own hide and get out of there. The others discovered he was not out there waiting for them when they came out and had run to a nearby grocery store parking lot and stole a car from there, and had made a getaway anyhow.

"Well, I can't call you 'Turley' anymore." Kylie said.

"You haven't been calling me 'Turley,' you have been calling me 'Turkey'."

"I'm sorry," Kylie said, "I'm sure that was irritating to you. I don't know what your name is, and I guess you don't either, so what shall I call you?"

"It wasn't irritating to me at all. You could call me anything you wanted to, and it would sound sweet to me as long as I knew you weren't calling me names because you were mad at me. You can just keep calling me 'Turkey' if you want to."

"Well, maybe your memory will return to you soon, and you will remember what your name is."

Kylie's expression became very serious, and she said, "I almost hope that you don't ever regain your memory, because I know that when you do you will probably be leaving, and I have got to where I really like having you around."

"Well, that door swings both ways," Turkey said just above a whisper, "I have got to where I totally enjoy being here with you, and I hate the thought of leaving, but I don't know if I have a family or just what my life was like before."

Turkey's expression was serious now too. "Sometimes for just a fleeting second I will think I am going to remember something, but just as quick as my memory is jogged it will be gone again. I don't know if I was about to remember something of my past, or if it was just an echo of my dreams. I feel so bewildered when I can't remember who I am or anything that has happened to me all my life."

Kylie could hardly believe what she had just heard. "Did he just say, 'an echo of my dreams?' she thought. "That is not an expression that is used a lot." But she remembered she had been thinking about the dreams she had about her and Carl that would have never come true, and she had felt that what she was starting to feel for Turkey was just echoes of those dreams. That was the expression she had used in her thoughts. "Well, they say great minds run in the same channels. Maybe it would be a little bit egotistical to think of our minds as great, but perhaps to think of two minds that are on the same level as running in the same channels would be alright." She thought.

Kylie felt very sympathetic, as she walked over and gave Turkey a hug.

"Whatever happens, I'll always remember you, and I will cherish this time I got to spend with you. I have never met anyone like you before. I'm so glad I got to meet you."

"Well, I am certainly glad I got to meet you. You rescued me. I don't know what I'd have done if you hadn't been here.

"Unless I have another memory lapse I'll never forget you either. I doubt that I have ever met anyone like you before either, but I can honestly say that I don't remember ever meeting anyone like you before."

Kylie smiled, and said, "I'm glad you can have a sense of humor about your loss of memory. I would probably be going crazy if it happened to me. And I apologize for not believing you."

"Well, I'll admit, when I woke up and didn't know who I was or where I was, or how I got there, I was pretty scared. I am very grateful to whoever it was, probably my parents, who taught me about God, and how to pray, because that was the first thing I thought to do. And you know how in the Bible when someone would talk about someone 'holding their peace'? That was sort of like we might say to someone to just 'stay calm', or 'keep your cool'. Well, when I prayed, all upset and scared, about to go out of my mind, it was sort of like God was saying to me, 'Just stay cool, I've got this.' And after that I felt at peace, and I wasn't afraid anymore. I decided that God was doing something that I didn't need to know about until He wants to reveal it to me."

Kylie sort of shook her head, and said, "Well, I guess that is some of the reason I thought you were making it up; you seemed awfully calm about something that would be enough to drive some people crazy."

Kylie set plates on the table and said, "Let's eat." and they sat down and asked the blessing, and went ahead with their meal.

While Kylie did the dishes and straightened up the kitchen, Turkey went and got the tools Kylie had told him about, and where to find them, and then went to check to see if he could discover what the problem with the pickup might be.

When Kylie finished, she came on out to see what progress Turkey was making.

"Your timing is perfect," Turkey said, "I wanted to show you this, if you can get down here where you can see it. These wires are in two, but they were not chewed in two by a rat or mouse. They were deliberately cut by someone."

"You mean that they weren't 'chewed' in two by a rat, they were 'cut' in two by a rat. I just can't imagine anyone doing such a thing," Kylie said sarcastically, "that is, except someone like Brackley or one of his men."

Turkey got the wires fastened back together, and said to Kylie, "Let's see if that is going to do the job. See if it will start."

The motor turned over a couple times and then started right up.

"That was the problem. I guess Brackley hadn't counted on someone being here to help you discover what he had done to bring you more grief."

Turkey brushed the dust out of his clothes and smiled at Kylie. "We will be watching for him, and maybe we can catch him in the act, and make it rough for him.

"I noticed you don't have any dog. If you had a dog to bark when someone came around it might be good." Turkey said.

"Well, that is another thing I didn't mention," Kylie said "we had two dogs, but they suspiciously died within a couple weeks of each other. I think they were poisoned."

"He is sounding more vicious all the time. We sure do need to come up with a plan to discourage him from the things he is doing."

They walked to the house, and Kylie suggested that Turkey take a shower, and then she said she would cut his hair for him. "I'll get you some of Carl's clothes to put on and I'll wash those for you since you have been wallowing in the dirt working on the pickup."

Turkey said that he liked that idea, and got started with the shower. When he finished Kylie told him to use the hair dryer and be sure his hair was good and dry.

Turkey enjoyed having Kylie comb and cut his hair. She fussed with it and talked about how it would look if it was cut this way, or maybe it would look better that way, but all the time it felt good to have her hands touching his head, and turning it this way and that way. He wished that it would take a lot longer than it did, but finally she was finished and held the mirror for him to see the results. He was surprised at the difference her haircut had made in the way he looked.

"Well, you are really something Kylie girl. That is a real nice job you did there. You made me look even better than I thought I could look."

"I told you that you would look better with a haircut." She said.

"And, as usual, you were right." Turkey replied.

"And if you can stay around long enough," said Kylie, " I'll feed you up good so that you aren't so skinny, and you will be a right handsome gentleman."

"Well now, when people go to fattening up a turkey, sometimes the turkey's future doesn't look very bright." Turkey joked.

Turkey was almost frightened of the feelings he had for Kylie. What would he do if he found that he was married and had children? His feelings for Kylie were so strong that at times he felt that he wouldn't be able to get along without her. He wasn't positively sure, but he felt that she also had feelings for him as well. He didn't have to think about it for long, because he knew what to do about it. It was time to pray.

"What can I do?" he asked God, and as before his answer came, "Stay cool, I've got this." Turkey reminded himself to just put it in the hands of The Lord. No one is capable of handling it better. With those thoughts he put it to rest, and went about taking care of the situation at hand.

"Well, what's next on the agenda?" he asked Kylie.

"I guess since the pickup is running now we could drive down to the mailbox and check to see if there are any bills for me to pay. And, tomorrow we could drive into town and I have bills there I need to pay, and I need to have the feed store bring me out some more alfalfa pellets to feed the cattle that I intend to get. I'll have them fill the silo that I auger it out of into the feed truck to feed the cattle. I'll need some more for this winter."

"I guess I'm about to get a good look at how a ranch is run."

Turkey thought, and it made him smile. He was veryimpressed with the way Kylie seemed so capable of handling things. She reminded him of what the Bible called the virtuous woman in Prov 31:10 where it says: "Who can find a virtuous woman? for her price is far above rubies." Then goes on to explain how capable of so much that a virtuous woman is able to handle. She would really be a prize for someone, and he thought that he would really be proud to be that someone.

They got in the pickup and Kylie drove down to the mailbox. There was nothing but an advertisement paper in the box. "Not worth the trip to get it." Kylie said.

"You want to drive on down to the bridge and see where the wreck happened?" Kylie asked.

"Yeah, I guess that would be okay. I saw it when I came by it the other day, but I was not in any shape to try to get a good look at it."

They drove down the highway to the bridge. Kylie parked the pickup off to the side of the road, and they walked over to the bridge.

As they walked onto the bridge Kylie pointed. "Whoever was driving when the wreck happened was driving way too fast when they hit the bridge. And the skid marks show that they suddenly turned and came clear across the highway and hit the left side of the bridge. The paper said the way things looked it appeared that something was distracting the driver. Otherwise it would appear that the wreck was intentional. That would have been crazy."

Turkey remembered the thing that was going through his mind when he woke up as though he was saying it, "I'm going to kill you. I'm going to kill all of you." And felt like he must have been in the wreck with them. But, he could not say anything to Kylie about it. He wondered if maybe they had taken him hostage and he had only heard one of them saying that during the robbery, but why did it seem so real that it was him saying it?

"Well, there are a lot of crazy drivers on the road; some of them sure don't have any business being there. That is why we have to watch their driving as well as our own when we get out on the road."

Turkey didn't say much more than that about what he saw. He was ready to go back to the house by the time Kylie was, so they went back to the ranch.

"Hey," Kylie said, "You haven't had time to look around at where I live yet. Come here, I want to show you something."

He followed her around to the back side of the house, and there not too very far away was a beautiful waterfall in the creek that rippled past the house.

"My grandpa built this house for Grandma, way back many years ago. "They went out riding around looking over the property after they bought it, and when Grandma saw this place she said she would like to have the house right here. I think it is the most beautiful place, don't you?"

"Wow," was all Turkey could say at first. But then he shook his head from side to side, and said, "It just couldn't have been built in a more beautiful spot. I love waterfalls and little creeks like this."

"And look at this," Kylie went on, "He built a back porch with a swing so that they could sit out here in the eveningsand listen to the water ripple down the creek."

"Wow," Turkey said again.

"I just couldn't help myself." He thought. "I have fallen in love with this girl that I have only known a few days, and now I've fallen in love with the ranch that she lives on."

"I could make up some iced tea, and we could sit out here and listen to the water if you'd like. Sometimes the bobwhite quail and the whippoorwills will be around and we might hear them too."

Turkey smiled. "Now how could I turn down an invitation like that? That sounds like the most pleasant thing a person could ever think of to do. It sounds wonderful."

Turkey sat in the porch swing just thinking of all that had taken place in the last few days, while Kylie went in to brew some tea.

Kylie soon came out with the iced tea and handed a glass to Turkey and sat down beside him. They sipped the tea and watched the sunset through the trees and listened to the ripple of the water.

"I can't imagine that I could have had a life as pleasant as this wherever it was that I came from." Turkey said.

"Well, it has been pleasant for me too, since you've been here." Kylie said. "Before that it was beginning to get pretty scary. Since you don't know who you are, you have no place to go to stay, and you have no job to earn money to get a place to stay, so why don't you stay here and maybe your memory will come back to you, and then you will be able to decide what to do?"

A whippoorwill began making its sound off in the distance, and then another answered back to it.

"But, I've got to say something," Kylie said, "and if you think I'm crazy you can tell me so, but I need to know what you think about it."

"Say away," Turkey said, "But, it would have to be something pretty wild before I could think of you as being crazy."

"Well, I know God's thoughts are so very far above our thoughts, and His ways are far above our ways, but sometimes if we are trying our best to do the things that He wants us to, I think we can get a glimpse of some of the things He is working out."

"I fully agree with that." Turkey said.

"And you said that when you woke up and couldn't remember who you were, or where you were, or how you got there you were frightened and you prayed, and you said it was like God said to you, 'Just stay cool, I've got this.' "

"That's right." Turkey answered.

"And you said that you felt peace come over you, and you just put everything in God's hands, and everything was okay after that."

"Right again," Turkey said, "But, I still hope He will let me know who I am before too long. I'm getting pretty anxious to find that out."

"Well, I had been praying for some help in my situation, with all the things that have been happening; things that I feel sure Brackley has been instigating. Then you showed up, and at least for a little while you sure put him on the run. Then you found the money that Granddad had saved up, and instead of taking it all for yourself, like you easily could have, you insisted that I keep it. I think God is using you to work out my problems, and maybe even using me to help you with problems in maybe helping you regain your memory, and possibly even some problems you don't even remember that you have right now."

"That could very well be." Said Turkey, "And I want you to know that I want to help you in every way that I can. You have helped me in ways that you could not even dream of, and mostly just by being a friend to me when I really needed one; and I still need you to be my friend."

Kylie reached over and put her hand on Turkey's hand.

"There is still something else I need to say. I understand that I have only known you two days, but I have started having feelings for you that I have never ever felt before for anyone, and I know that I can't let myself entertain those feelings, because you might be married and it could get me a great big heartbreak in the end. I saw that you are not wearing a wedding ring, but I can see that you have worn one at some time, because there is lighter colored skin around your finger where a ring used to be. It might be that if someone robbed you like you said might have happened, then they may have even took your wedding ring. But, there could be other reasons you don't have one now. Anyway, you might not ever be able to feel the same about me, but I need you to make me back away if I get to acting too affectionate.

Turkey interrupted her before she said more. "As far as me ever feeling the same about you goes, I already do, and I have been having those same thoughts, so we will just have to help each other, because I don't like heartbreaks any more than you do. If I am married I don't want to do my wife wrong, because I wouldn't want to hurt her either."

"I'm glad you understand," Kylie said. "I didn't know how to talk to you about this, but it was easier than I thought it would be. Thank you for being so understanding."

"Well, we've been in constant company with each other for these past couple days; we may find it easier to think about other things when we have to be away from each other."

Turkey said.

"Probably so," Kylie answered.

CHAPTER FIVE: Going to town

The next morning was partly cloudy at first, but the skies soon cleared and as Kylie and Turkey prepared to go to town they checked to be sure all the doors were locked. "I sure don't want anyone going in the house while we're gone." Kylie said.

"It would be just like Brackley to be watching to see when we leave so that he could come around and snoop."

As they walked toward the pickup Kylie turned to Turkey and asked, "Do you want to drive?"

"I don't have any driver's license." Turkey answered.

"Oh, that's right. Well, you can drive the feed truck around on the ranch."

"Well, riding a horse is fine with me. I can pretend that I'm a real cowboy."

"But, there will be places that we will need to take tools and fence repairs that we can't haul when we are riding horses." Kylie replied.

"Oh, you've been thinking up things to do to put me to work."

"Well, these things have been on my mind from before the time you showed up. I have had a few days that I got sidetracked from my work, but maybe with you helping me I can get caught up again."

"Well, I am more than happy to be here to help you out. I might be a little bit slow at first because of my gimpy leg, but it is quite a lot better today than it was yesterday. But you may have to be patient with me if I am slow at learning to do the work."

"Oh, you'll do fine," said Kylie, "you rode the horse like an old hand, and you did the fence work like a pro; you must have done this kind of work before. If you haven't, there really isn't that much to it; you'll catch on fast."

"I think it will be fun." Turkey said, "Just being with you is a lot of fun, so what ever work there is in it will be okay."

Kylie smiled, but didn't say anything more. She was turning onto the main highway now, and started picking up speed.

As they rode along Kylie pointed out different things along the way, and told about where different people lived. It was interesting to Turkey, even though he told Kylie he didn't think he would be able to remember much of it. He joked about not having a real good memory, and Kylie laughed.

After they had been quite a while on the road Turkey asked, "How far is it to town?"

"Well, there are a couple smaller towns kinda off in the other direction, but, where we are going is about forty five miles. It is a bigger town, and has a few more places that I need to do business without having to go to one town to do one kind of business, and then go all the way to the other town to do another kind of business."

Turkey was fascinated with Kylie, and enjoyed just hearing her talk. "I understand," he said.

"It is nearly time to eat." Kylie said. "If we eat now we can get in before noon when everyone else shows up, and we won't have to wait so long for our food."

"Makes good sense to me," Turkey said. "Do they have some pretty good places to eat here?"

"Well, they used to have, but it has been a very long time since I have eaten in town. Carl never took me with him when he went to town, so unless I went with Granddad I just didn't come in to town."

"I guess we can find out if they are any better or any worse than they used to be." Turkey said.

They parked the pickup as close to the cafe as possible, but they still had to walk quite a ways to get to the cafe. As they walked down the street Kylie suddenly stopped and looked down at the headlines on a paper that was for sale in a newspaper rack.

"Well, just let me see what this is all about." Kylie said as she deposited the money for a newspaper.

"What is it?" Turkey asked.

"I shouldn't be happy about this, but I guess I am happy because if they nail him he won't be doing all these things to other people."

"What is it?" Turkey asked again.

"It says here that Brackley is being investigated for several of his underhanded business dealings. It seems that he got a little bit careless, and slipped up; then tried to have one of his men take the rap for him, and some of his other hired hands got with that one and stood against Brackley. It doesn't look too good for Brackley. He may be important enough to get away with a lot of things, but if God is ready for him to get caught, he is not going to get away with his crooked dealings any more."

"But just look at all the people that are affected by peoplelike him who deal so maliciously. Some suffer some real lossand hurt, and some are people who are trying to do what is right." Turkey answered and began walking again following Kylie as she resumed her stride down the sidewalk.

"Yes," Kylie said, "Grandpa said that we all go through times when we are tested to see just what our reaction to the way we are treated is going to be. God uses people like him at times, but there are many other ways that we are tried to see if we will blame God for our hard luck and quit trusting Him, or if we will keep holding on to our faith in God through it all. But, if we are trying to serve God we can be sure the enemy is going to be after us to try to make us fall. We need to have plenty of the Holy Spirit to give us the strength to stand. Grandpa said he knew some people who were afraid to turn to the Lord because of the scripture that says that all that will live godly in Christ Jesus shall suffer persecution. He said that they just didn't feel like they would be able to handle the persecution. But, none of us could in our own strength. We have to have the strength of The Holy Spirit within us.

"Grandpa said he didn't know why people who trust in God sometimes have a very rough time in life. He said there were a lot of times he saw some of the most sincere Christians and those who were what he would consider being the best Christians that were having the hardest struggles in life. Many people would say that they must not be living right or they would not be having such a hard time; but he didn't believe that. He believed they would have greater rewards for standing strong through the tests and trials they were going through. God knows how much we can handle, and He will not allow bigger trials than what we can handle to ever overtake us. He has also promised us that He will never leave us or forsake us, so He will be right there to help us through anything that comes along. Those who pass the hardest tests will receive the greatest rewards, Grandpa said. He said that I will have tests to go through, and I should really put my faith and trust in God, because that would make me strong."

Turkey and Kylie talked more about this as they sat eating their lunch. Turkey was very impressed with Kylie's knowledge about so many different things, but most of all her knowledge of the Bible and spiritual things.

"How did you get so smart about everything?" Turkey asked. "Well, I'm not trying to pat myself on the back, but Ifeel like I have learned quite a few things. I guess Grandma and Grandpa kept me studying because they wanted me to not be a dummy or naive when I grew up. They said that if I didn't know some of these things I would be vulnerable to all sorts of different treachery and deceitfulness in the world. If it hadn't been for them teaching me certain things I would have fallen for Carl's lies even more than I did, and then I'd have been so much more of a conflict for Grandpa about selling the ranch."

"Brackley must have wanted the ranch pretty badly to have gone to so much trouble as you've told me he did to get it."

"I think it was his ego that made him so obsessed and so determined to get the property. He just couldn't stand to be told no when he tried to buy it from Granddad. He did make Granddad a pretty decent offer, but it was worth more to Grandpa to keep the property than what the money amounted to. He said that he would never find a ranch that had

everything that he had with this one, and that is probably another reason Brackley wants it so bad. I think he is hooked on power and control the way someone gets hooked on drugs. It is just another way the enemy has of taking someone further and further if they ever yield to temptations that are put before them.

"But, even Grandpa was kind of fooled at first, and thought it was a good thing that Brackley was buying up all the property around us. "Grandpa said that would keep too many people from moving in too close, 'cause Grandpa liked being not real close to neighbors. He said that privacy is worth a lot, and once you lose it you won't be able to get it back. But then we learned that Brackley planned to divide all the acreage up and sell to people who wanted to just have a few acres to build on, so it looks like there will be lots of people all around us anyway; but at least Grandpa won't have to see it happen."

"But, you have quite a few acres, so even if people do move in on what Brackley sells them, you will still be where they are not right up against you aren't you?"

"Yeah, and Grandpa built the house right in the middle of the ranch, so even if they are right up against the property line, they will still be pretty far away from the house,"

Turkey reached over and put his hand on Kylie's hand.

"Well, what the paper was telling about that is happening to Brackley will probably slow him down a bit, and what you said about him not being able to get away with these things if God wants to stop him is absolutely true. And I wanted to say something about that. When we were talking on the back porch you said something about me really putting Brackley on the run at least for a while. I took the credit for it at the time because it made me feel good to hear it, but it was God who just used me to put him on the run. I am still proud that God used me to do it, but God gets the credit for doing it,"

Kylie's eyes filled with tears, and she said, "You and I think so much alike, I am so glad that God brought you around forme to meet you. I just pray that it is God's plan for you to stay around. But, if it isn't, I want you to know that it is such a joy to get to know you as much as I have. You are quite a man, Turkey who ever you are."

"Well you are quite a girl, Kylie, what ever your last name is, and it is joy to get to know you too. I am just putting my life in God's hands, and the Bible says all things work together for good for those who love The Lord, and are called according to His purpose."

"Then we can expect good things to happen, can't we?" Kylie answered.

Kylie and Turkey finished their meal and were going back to the pickup to go to the different businesses they would need to, and as they were walking along the sidewalk someone called out to Kylie. "Hey Girl, how've you been? I haven't seen you for a while."

As Kylie turned to see who was addressing her, the man walked up beside her.

"Oh, hi Doug," Kylie answered, "Well, I don't make it to town very often lately; been pretty busy trying to keep up with the work."

"I can understand that," replied Doug, "there's always more work than there is time to do it in isn't there?" Then Doug abruptly changed the subject.

"I'll bet you haven't met the new kid the pet store hired yet have you? I like to give him a bad time. Come on in if you have time and we'll see if we can get a good laugh out of him."

Kylie and Turkey followed Doug into the pet store.

"Hi," Doug greeted the new sales clerk. "Tell me about that new spray for your dogs and cats that is being advertised."

"Oh, you must mean this right here." the clerk said as he walked back and took an item from the shelf.

"This has a lot more flea and tick protection than nearly all the other brands."

"Do you have some that doesn't protect the fleas and ticks? 'cause I don't want to protect them. They are what I want to get rid of." Doug said as he winked at Kylie.

"Oh, that is what the flea and tick protection is, Sir, it protects your pet from the fleas and ticks, it doesn't protect the fleas and ticks." And the clerk went on to give a long and detailed explanation of the meaning of flea and tick protection.

"Well, if you are absolutely sure it's not going to protect the fleas and ticks, I'll go ahead and buy some." Doug said.

Kylie and Turkey smiled at Doug, and Kylie gave him a thumbs up sign, and said, "Good to see you Doug." and they went on out of the store.

"I was afraid that Doug was going to ask me to introduce you to him," Kylie said, "and I didn't know just how to introduce someone that I didn't even know their name. I didn't think there was any chance that I would see anyone that I knew here in town, but, I'm glad you got to catch that in the pet store. Doug is a clown in the sense that he likes to joke around with people. I can tell you his name; it is Doug Thorn. I went to school with him. But, I wouldn't have known what to tell him about you if he had asked. I am glad that he is not a nosey sort of person. I think he figured that I would introduce you to him if I wanted to, but he would give me the choice of when and how to do it."

"You handled that situation pretty smooth." Turkey said, "But that makes me think; if it just so happens that I am from here, and someone that knows me, and sees me with you, and tells my wife about it, if it happens to be that I am married, then I may find myself in trouble. But, I guess I'll cross that bridge when and if I come to it."

Kylie nodded and said, "We both may have bridges to cross up ahead that we can't even imagine are there right now." And they walked on down the sidewalk.

Kylie had quite a few places to go, and things to do, so the afternoon was passing quickly. Finally she said to Turkey, "Is there anything you need while we are here? I think I have completed all my shopping, and bill paying."

"I can't think of a thing." Turkey answered. So they got into the pickup, and started toward the ranch.

CHAPTER SIX: What can you tell me about this man?

Just as they were getting to the edge of town, not quite to where they got on to the main highway, Turkey started saying very loudly, "Stop! Stop! Stop the pickup!"

And as soon as Kylie barely came to a stop he was out of the pickup, and running.

Kylie was going to ask him what the matter was, but he was gone out of hearing distance before she could.

When she looked beyond where he was at, and to where he was running to she could see there was a house on fire about a block away.

She put the pickup in gear and backed up, then drove on around the corner to where she was closer to where the burning house was. She wondered what was going on. Why was he going to where the burning house was?

She got out of the pickup and walked on closer to the burning house. There were other people gathering around to look.

She didn't see Turkey, or where he had gone.

Someone, not talking to anyone in particular said, "He went in the house; he is liable to get burned up too,"

Kylie wasn't sure if it was Turkey who had gone in the house or someone else, but she didn't see Turkey anywhere, so she decided it must have been Turkey that the person was talking about.

"Why would he do that?" she wondered. She could hear the sirens of the fire trucks that were now arriving. Someone had called the fire department. The firemen were hurrying around, and someone was telling them that a man had gone into the building, and hadn't come out yet. The house was being consumed by the fire very quickly, and it didn't look like anyone was going to go into the building with it so far gone.

It was determined that there was a woman and her young son inside the building, but it was too late to try to save them.

Someone else now said that a man had gone into the building,

and still hadn't come out yet.

Kylie was crying, and praying, and wondering why Turkey would do what he did.

Just then turkey came out of the building half carrying, and half dragging the woman in one arm, and with the other hand he had the arm of the young boy, and was bringing him out too. Turkey barely got out the door of the building and collapsed. The woman was still conscious and was worried about her son, asking if he was alright. She said that she had tried to get him out, but it took so long to find him in all the smoke that by the time she found him he was overcome by the smoke. She said that she couldn't find her way out because of the thick smoke, but she had heard the man calling for Gina and somebody else. She said she didn't know who they were or why he was calling those names, but she had answered, and he came and got them both or they would not have made it out.

The three of them were taken to the hospital, and were being treated for burns and smoke inhalation. Kylie followed them to the hospital.

It seemed like it was going to take forever before she would be able to find out anything about Turkey. Some of the other people were getting news about the woman and her son, and it seemed that they were going to be alright except for burns that were not terribly bad, but would take a while to heal. Kylie heard someone say that it was a miracle that they had even been able to get out of the burning building, but an extra miracle that they didn't have more burns than they had.

When she asked about Turkey again, someone came up and asked her, "What can you tell me about this man? He says he can't remember who he is, or where he is from. Can you tell me about him?"

"No, I don't know him by name," Kylie said, "I just befriended him, but he had lost his memory before I met him,"

Someone came up to the man who was asking Kylie about Turkey, and told him that someone had seen his picture on TV when it was showing him coming out of the burning building bringing the woman and her son out, and had recognized him as someone that had turned up missing a few days ago, and they had called and said they would be there in about three and a half or four hours.

Kylie thought finally she was going to find out who he was, but she wondered if it was going to be a good thing or a bad thing that she would find out.

Turkey had been asking to have Kylie come into his room to see him, so she got to visit with him while they waited.

Kylie went to the side of the bed where Turkey was, and gave him a hug.

"That was a brave thing you did, but how did you know they were in there? Did you know those people?"

"It is something strange to me that I don't understand." Turkey said. "It was like I was in a different time, but I seemed to understand what I was doing when it was happening. I just felt like I had to get them out. I thought I knew them when I went in searching for them, and I thought I knew them when I was getting them out. I was so thankful that I had found them and managed to get them out; but then when we got out of the

house, I had no idea who they were."

Kylie was holding Turkey's hand as they talked. "I didn't know what it was all about when you ran to the burning house like you did. I thought perhaps you knew the people that lived there."

"When I saw the house burning I had a picture of a house and a neighborhood in my mind. The street was the same, the drive to the house seemed the same, and that was how it looked to me until after we got out of the house, but after we were out, and I got a look at everything, it didn't look anything like the picture I had in my mind. But, I feel like my memory got a good jolt, and I am going to keep working on that picture that I had in my mind, because I think it is a picture of something that is part of my past."

Kylie patted Turkey's hand and said, "I was so worried about you inside that burning building. It seemed like forever waiting for you to come out. I am so glad you didn't have more burns, and that you didn't suffer more from breathing all that smoke."

"Yeah, I'm glad it is all over with, but I'll be even gladder when all these news people will leave me alone. They will be back to get the rest of the story as soon as this guy and his wife that say they know me get here to reveal to them who I am.

"But, I am just as anxious if not more so than the news people are to find out who I am."

It was just a little longer than four hours before the man who had called finally showed up. The news people kept him busy for a long time, so it was even longer that Kylie and Turkey had to wait to meet the man and his wife that said they knew him.

The man turned out to be the pastor where Turkey had gone to church, and when he walked into the room he said, "Well, hello Luke, it seems you have become quite a hero. You were all over the news about the mystery man who couldn't remember who he was, but turned up to save a woman and her son."

Turkey looked up and studied the man, but didn't seem to recognize him.

"Do you not remember me?" The man asked.

"When you said, 'Luke,' that sounds familiar, and so does your voice. If I was to see you in your usual surroundings it might help; but yes, I think I am beginning to remember a little bit."

The pastor turned to Kylie, and asked her what she had been calling him, and she told him the story of how she had begun calling him 'Turkey,' and the pastor laughed. "Well, let me introduce you to Luke Remington. He happens to be a very good friend of mine, and he helps me out quite a lot in the church. I can always count on him to fill in for me if I need to take time off for some reason. I'm a little bit wary of letting it happen too often though, because the congregation likes to hear him preach as well as they do me, so I don't want to come back and find that they want him all the time instead of me."

Luke had a curios look on his face as the pastor talked, as though the sound of his voice and his mannerism was starting to jog his memory some.

The pastor continued, "Kylie was talking about you coming up to her place just a short time after the robbery, and that is strange that the robbery was right close to where you lived.

"The car that they stole was from the parking lot of the grocery store just walking distance from your place. After she was telling about you being near where she lives just shortly after the time that they had the wreck on the bridge, it seems that there could be a chance that they took you hostage, and had you with them, and that may be how you ended up right there at that time."

"I remember that parking lot," Luke said. "I remember what happened now too. These things are coming back to me in a rush. I was walking over to the grocery store to get me something to snack on, and there was this old lady who was having problems with getting her walker out of her car, and I was going over to see if I could help her. She managed to get it out and started to the store before I could get there. But she had left her car door open. I hollered at her that she had left the car door open, but I guess she was hard of hearing, so I just went up to close the door for her, and I noticed that she had also left the keys in the ignition. I thought that I would just get the keys, and close the door, and take her keys to her in the store, when three guys walked up and stuck a gun in my ribs and told me to get in the car. I didn't feel like I could win any argument with a gun, so I did as I was told.

"They made me drive, and they seemed to know just where to go to dodge the police. I guess since the lady who owned the car didn't realize for some time that her car was even missing, it gave them time to get a good head start.

They made me give them my billfold and after they took everything out of it, they threw it out the window. One of them wanted to keep my credit cards, but the other two said they didn't want to use them because that would leave a trail that could show where they were. But they took everything I had in my pockets. I didn't understand why they wanted everything, but I soon realized they planned to kill me, and they wanted to remove any clue they could so as not to leave a trail. They were going to try to slow the law down in finding anything that would indicate which way they went. But they made me give them my wedding ring for whatever it might bring as something to hock for money."

When Luke mentioned his wedding ring Kylie felt a twinge of hurt in her heart, and almost a sob wanting to come out, but she hid it as best she could.

Luke took a drink of coffee that had been brought to him, and continued with the story. "All the while they were cursing the one that they called Turley for leaving just to save him self when the police started getting there, but I'll bet any one of the other three would have done the same thing. They mentioned killing him and dumping him over a bridge somewhere a couple times, so when we saw a bridge up ahead, and they told me to stop on the bridge because they had to get rid of some excess baggage, I knew they were talking about me. I felt sure that I was going to die anyway, so I felt like I might at least be able to get them stranded there to slow them down for the police, if not put a stop to their robbing for good, so I just pushed the accelerator to the floor, and I told them I was going to kill all of them. I told them that I knew they had intended to kill me, but I was going to kill them instead. I kept telling them over and over again.

"When I woke up by the river, I still had, 'I'm going to kill you,' going through my mind. I told them that this is what their kind of life had brought them to. It never crossed my mind that I would live through it, and especially I didn't think that I would come out of it with no more damage to me than I got.

"The one in the front seat beside me started kicking my right leg with the heel of his shoe, trying to make me get my foot off the accelerator, but I wouldn't do it. They were all cursing me, and the one in the back seat behind me grabbed my hair and pulled my head back where I couldn't see where I was going, but I was able to judge just about when to turn and hit the bridge. I don't know how fast we were going when I hit the bridge, but it was fast enough to do the job. The next thing I remember was waking up along the river down stream from the bridge, and when I woke up I couldn't remember anything. As long as I have gone without being able to remember, and now it all just came back to me in a flash. I almost can't believe that I couldn't remember."

The pastor shook his head and said, "Wow that is some story, Luke. We were all praying for you, and now God has brought you back to us safe and well. Here comes my wife, She probably has you all checked out, so we are almost ready to go. You can ride with us, and we'll take you home, but just for a bit I need to talk to you about your wife and son."

When the pastor said that, Kylie felt like she was just not ready for this, and might start crying. As brightly as she could manage she said, "I hate to rush off like this, but I need to get back to the ranch and get to bed so I can get some sleep. Tomorrow I need to get started on some work that needs to be done. It was real nice to meet you and your wife, Pastor.

"You'll have to have Luke bring you all over to the ranch, and we'll have a big picnic and barbecue sometime."

"That sounds great." The pastor said, as Kylie went and gave Luke a hug before she left. "You take care, now Turkey, and don't forget me. I'll never forget you."

"I sure don't want to have anymore memory lapses," Luke said, "But unless I do there is no chance I'll ever forget you. Are you sure you can't stay just a little longer?"

"No, I really need to get on back to the ranch," Kylie said.

"Keep me in your prayers, you'll be in mine."

And with that Kylie was out the door and gone. She sobbed all the way to the pickup, and when she got in the pickup she leaned her head on the steering wheel and prayed and cried.

Then, as if God was speaking to her, she remembered what Luke had told her about how it was almost as if God had spoken to him, and said, 'just keep cool, I've got this.'

Kylie raised her head up, and brushed the tears from her eyes and said, "Yes, Lord, I know this is all in your hands, and your Word says that all things work together for good for those who love you, and I truly do love you Lord, and I am thankful that I got to meet Luke, and you worked through Him to help me in so many ways. I pray for him and his family that you will just keep them in your care, and bless them for Luke being such a blessing to me."

Echoes Of My Dreams

CHAPTER SEVEN: Just stay cool, I've got this

It seemed so lonesome on the ranch now with Luke not there. The loneliness hung so heavy that it hurt. Kylie just couldn't get her mind on anything, and just sort of stumbled through the next several days. She just wasn't able to get any of the work done that she had indicated that she needed to get back to the ranch to do.

Over and over again she would ask herself how it was possible to fall so deeply and desperately in love with someone she had only known for a few days. She knew it hadn't been love at first sight, because when she first saw him she thought he looked just like someone would look who was involved in the things it appeared that he was involved with.

His appearance was of someone who had paid no attention to the way he appeared to other people, as if he was getting in their face daring anyone to say anything about how he looked. It was an appearance that she could never be attracted to, but yet as she knew him a little more as time went by, her attitude towards him had changed.

She did admit though, that when he fell face first in the cow manure she felt sorry for him. Perhaps that was when it started, and it just gradually kept growing more and more into a fondness for him, even though she was on guard to make sure that was something that didn't happen. But it eventually happened anyway, and then that fondness began to be admiration when she began seeing the kind of character he had. She had been on guard then too, because she didn't want to be taken in by someone pretending to be what they were not. But, now it had pretty well been proven that he was just the kind of man she would really like to have around all the time, but that was impossible, because he was already married.

Each time she prayed she asked God why it had seemed just like it was something that truly should be, and why she had not been able to keep herself from believing that it just had to be His will. She began to wonder if she would ever be the same after meeting Luke. She would never have believed that anyone could have that much impact on another person.

"I've got to pull myself together and get over this." She told herself. "If I don't, I'll be worse off than when I was worried and wondering what the next trick Brackley was going to pull on me."

A few more days drug by, and Kylie forced herself to get out and fix fence and a few other odds and ends jobs, but she was still lonely in the evenings, and remembered having conversations with Luke, and how it had just seemed so right.

"I just didn't care if there was anyone else in the world but him and me." She thought. "I don't think I could ever get bored being around him. I hope his wife realizes what a prize she has in him, and treats him right."

Kylie resolved to give it all to God, although it was not real easy to do, and get on with life, so each morning she planned out her day and tried to stay busy so she wouldn't have time to think about things that she had no control over.

She was out in the chicken house gathering eggs one morning when a car drove up into the yard.

When Kylie came out to see who had come to visit, she saw that it was Luke.

"Well, hello Turkey," she said. "It is good to see you. You didn't forget me after all, did you?"

She didn't know just how to act now that she knew for sure that he was married. She wanted to rush over and hug his neck, but she didn't feel that would be an acceptable action, so she forced herself to be more standoffish and cool.

Luke acted real formal, in a joking sort of way, as though he already knew the answer she would give for what he was about to ask her.

"I wanted to see if you might be able to use a ranch hand around here." Luke said. "I have had lots of experience. I grew up on my uncle's ranch and learned how to do most everything concerning ranch work. In fact I have been saving my money since I was fifteen years old, hoping to buy a ranch of my own some day, so If you could use a ranch hand I'd like to apply for the job."

"Oh, this would never work." Kylie thought. "Even worse than having Luke not being around, would be having him around with his wife and son." She purposely ignored what he had just said, and asked, "How have you been? And how are your wife and son? I'll bet they were glad to have you back."

Now Luke's demeanor changed. "I guess you didn't read the newspaper."

"Well, I haven't done much reading lately, I didn't look at the mail or the paper when I got them. I just tossed them into a drawer and thought I'd look at them some other time." Kylie said slowly.

"Well, I'll bring you up to date about some things." Luke said as he walked over closer to Kylie.

"Sometime back, before the robbery took place, I had been working nights, and I came home from work one morning and found my house was on fire. I tried to rush in and find my wife and son, but there were already people gathered there and there were fire trucks there, and the people held me back and wouldn't let me go in. I lost my wife and son in that fire.

"When you and I were passing that house that was on fire, it was to me just so much like it was my house again.

Everything was very much the same, and that is why I ran to it and rushed in and got the lady and her son out. It wasn't bravery on my part, or me trying to be a hero; it was in my mind that it was my wife and my son. But when I lost my wife and son I lost the will to live after that. I kept wishing that I had gone in the house and died with them. I couldn't go back to work, I couldn't sleep, and I didn't have any appetite, so I hardly ate any food at all. That is why I was so gaunt and grubby when I got here and found you. My weakness and passing out was not so much from being hurt in the wreck on the bridge, it was more that my system was just so run down, and because I hadn't slept for so long, my body was trying to recuperate from the loss of sleep, and from not eating.

"The pastor and his wife had rented an apartment for me right close to the grocery store that I was going to when the robbery took place. I hadn't eaten anything for I don't know how long, and I was getting pretty weak. I had decided I needed to eat something, so I thought I would walk over to the grocery store and get some kind of snack. That is when I saw the older lady leaving her car with the door open, and the keys in the ignition. It was truly a blessing to me that those thugs made me drive them to where I could meet you. I didn't

91

care at that time if I did die in the wreck. But then, with so much devastation, my mind just blotted out all the hurtful memories that I had until I could get acquainted with you. It made me to where I would be able to see that life didn't just stop altogether when I lost my family. I truly loved my wife and son, and I know it would have nearly been impossible for me to find another love as long as I had any memories of them. But the way things happened, and the way God was working things out; just like you said you thought He was doing when we were talking that time; I had no memories of them while I was getting to know you. It was hard for me again after I started remembering, and it took quite a lot of time, and a lot of counseling from my pastor to really deal with it after I got back and all the memories came back to me.

But I also had the memories of you, and when my pastor found out how I felt about you it gave him another approach for counseling me. He got through to me a lot better to make me realize that I can go on with life after losing my wife and son.

I think that even though I will always remember my wife and son, and will always love them, those memories won't get in the way of me loving you now, if you think you could love me, and let me love you after all that."

Kylie dropped the eggs she had gathered, and nearly flew to Luke and threw her arms around his neck and kissed him as she had wanted to do so many times before. With tears flowing down her face she said, "You know, I do think I could use a hired hand around here, and I think the opportunity for a quick promotion to a much higher position, like maybe 'General Manager' is quite possible."

THE END

www.ingramcontent.com/pod-product-compliance
Lightning Source LLC
Chambersburg PA
CBHW070520130626
46555CB00003B/1293

* 9 7 8 0 9 9 0 8 0 3 4 8 5 *